The man could kiss. The wildness that Olivia had suspected lay under his controlled exterior? She'd just had a taste of it! And it had left her mind whirling and her lips—and other parts of her body—throbbing.

Bemused, Olivia followed Ben towards the limo. She barely heard the shouts of the reporters or saw the flashbulbs going off.

She'd never been kissed like that before. She'd hardly been kissed at all.

Not, of course, that she was going to tell Ben that.

But it had been some kiss. And one she'd wanted, had been thinking about all night. Even longer, if she were honest with herself. And when the reporters had asked for a kiss...well, Olivia hadn't been about to say no. She'd wanted to kiss him too much, and the request was no more than an excuse to touch him. Taste him.

And he'd tasted good.

She slid into the limo, saw that Ben was sitting with his face turned determinedly towards the window.

Olivia thought about making some wry comment about the kiss, joking about it even, but she couldn't quite make herself do it. The kiss had been wonderful, but the way he'd thrust her away from him afterwards...

Well, that had been a little ego-bruising. She wasn't sure why he'd done it, and she didn't think she could pull off the breezy confidence to ask. Not when she had so little experience with kisses, and especially kisses like that.

The world's most elite hotel is looking for a jewel in its crown, and Spencer Chatsfield has found it. But Isabella Harrington, the girl from his past, refuses to sell!

Now the world's most decadent destinations have become a chessboard in this game of power, passion and pleasure...

Welcome to

The Chatsfield

Synonymous with style, sensation...and scandal!

With the eight Chatsfield siblings happily married and settling down, it's time for a new generation of Chatsfields to shine.

Spencer Chatsfield steps in as CEO, determined to prove his worth. But when he approaches Isabella Harrington, of Harringtons Boutique hotels, with the offer of a merger that would benefit them both...he's left with a stinging red palm-shaped mark on his cheek!

And so begins a game of cat and mouse that will shape the future of the Chatsfields and the Harringtons forever.

But neither knows that there's one stakeholder with the power to decide their fates...and the identity will shock both the Harringtons *and* the Chatsfields.

Just who will come out on top?

Find out in

Maisey Yates—**Sheikh's Desert Duty**

Abby Green—**Delucca's Marriage Contract**

Carol Marinelli—**Princess's Secret Baby**

Kate Hewitt—**Virgin's Sweet Rebellion**

Caitlin Crews—**Greek's Last Redemption**

Michelle Conder—**Russian's Ruthless Demand**

Susanna Carr—**Tycoon's Delicious Debt**

Melanie Milburne—**Chatsfield's Ultimate Acquisition**

8 titles to collect—you won't want to miss out!

Kate Hewitt

Virgin's Sweet Rebellion

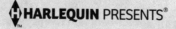

ISBN-13: 978-0-373-13804-3

Virgin's Sweet Rebellion

First North American publication 2015

Copyright © 2015 by Harlequin Books S.A.

Special thanks and acknowledgment are given to Kate Hewitt for
her contribution to The Chatsfield series.

Recycling programs
for this product may
not exist in your area.

Printed in U.S.A.

www.Harlequin.com

After spending three years as a die-hard New Yorker, **Kate Hewitt** now lives in a small village in the English Lake District with her husband, their five children and a golden retriever. In addition to writing intensely emotional stories, she loves reading, baking and playing chess with her son—she has yet to win against him, but she continues to try. Learn more about Kate at kate-hewitt.com.

Books by Kate Hewitt
Harlequin Presents

Kholodov's Last Mistress
Undoing of De Luca

Rivals of the Crown of Kadar
Captured by the Sheikh
Commanded by the Sheikh

The Diomedi Heirs
The Prince She Never Knew
A Queen for the Taking?

The Bryants: Powerful & Proud
Beneath the Veil of Paradise
In the Heat of the Spotlight
His Brand of Passion

The Power of Redemption
The Darkest of Secrets
The Husband She Never Knew

Visit the Author Profile page
at Harlequin.com for more titles.

To Suzy Clarke—thanks for being
such a great editor.

PROLOGUE

'YOU KNEW.' BEN CHATSFIELD stared at his brother Spencer and tried to suppress the sudden surge of rage that threatened to overwhelm him. His hands clenched into fists at his sides and words—angry, bitter words—bubbled to his lips. He swallowed them down. He swallowed it all down, as he always had, and gave a wry quirk of a smile, as if Spencer's revelation was nothing more than amusing. 'So. How long have you known?'

'That I was illegitimate?' Spencer's mouth tightened and he gave a little shrug. 'Five years. Since my twenty-ninth birthday.'

Five years. Ben blinked as he tried to take that in. For the past five *years* he'd been estranged from his brother, from his whole family, and for what?

For nothing apparently.

'It's a nice place you've got here,' Spencer offered, and Ben didn't answer. Spencer gazed round the relaxed yet elegant dining room of

Ben's flagship bistro in Nice, where he'd shown up out of the blue, walking through the tinted glass doors, his sunglasses slid onto his forehead, as if he were for all the world just another tourist.

Not Ben's older brother, the leader of their Three Musketeers, once adored, always missed. When Ben had rounded the corner from the kitchen and come to a standstill, Spencer had smiled easily, as if they'd seen each other last week instead of fourteen years ago.

'Hey, Ben,' he'd said, and somehow Ben had found his voice and answered back, his voice clipped.

'Spencer.'

And now his brother was telling him that he'd known for five years the secret Ben had discovered when he was just eighteen years old, the secret that had broken his heart and forced him to leave home, severing all ties with his family. The secret that had cost him so much, maybe even his own soul, and still Spencer just smiled.

'It's old history now, Ben,' he said, and Ben could tell Spencer was trying to be conciliatory. Five years too late. 'Water under the bridge. I always knew there was something that made Michael treat me differently from you and James, and I'm just glad I finally found out it was because he always knew I wasn't his biological son. I've made peace with that.'

'Glad you have,' Ben answered. He kept his voice even despite the tangle of emotion that had lodged in his chest: regret and guilt, sorrow and happiness at seeing his beloved brother again, but one trumped all the others. Anger.

The old anger still burned red-hot, a molten river inside him, boiling over everything. So Spencer thought he could just stroll back into Ben's life as if he'd never left. No apologies, no explanations, just a waving aside of fourteen years.

'What are you doing here, Spencer?' Ben asked, and his brother raised his eyebrows, looking slightly startled at Ben's flat tone, the blunt question.

'Aren't you glad? It's been a long time, Ben...'

'You've known where I've been.'

'You've known where I've been,' Spencer countered. and Ben stared at him evenly.

'I didn't know that you knew the truth.'

'Would that have made a difference?' Spencer asked, his eyes narrowing, and Ben flicked his gaze away.

'Maybe.' Would he have come back into the Chatsfield fold if he'd known Spencer knew about his bastard birth? Hard to say. He didn't have a lot of happy memories of being a Chatsfield. 'So you haven't actually answered the question,' he told Spencer. 'What are you doing here?'

Because he was realising, with another white-hot shaft of anger, that Spencer had only come looking for him because he wanted something from him.

'I decided it was time to reunite the Three Musketeers,' Spencer said. 'James is in Nice too, just for the weekend, and he wants to see you. We can finally all be together again, Ben, for the good of The Chatsfield.'

The Chatsfield. The hotel empire that his father had lived for, that would have been Spencer's legacy if he hadn't been illegitimate. Except, of course, it *was* his legacy, because their uncle Gene had agreed to let Spencer step up as CEO after their cousin Lucilla had resigned. Ben had heard that much through the news at least. He tried not to read anything about The Chatsfield, but bits of news still reached him.

And now it seemed Spencer wanted Ben to work for the *good* of The Chatsfield. Fall in with his plans as if half of their lives hadn't been spent apart.

'You don't care about reuniting the Three Musketeers,' he told his brother, a sneer entering his voice. 'Give me a break, Spencer. What you really want is for me to do something for you. For The Chatsfield. Don't you?'

Spencer drew back, surprised and perhaps affronted. *I'm not the brother he remembers*, Ben thought. The puppyish, eager to please brother who had tried to make everyone so damn happy, and had always failed. Failed spectacularly. He was done with that, done with pleasing other people for no real purpose. And he wasn't about to work for Spencer or The Chatsfield.

'I'm a little busy already, as you can see,' he told Spencer, lightening his words with another wry smile. Joking was his default, the better and easier option than what he really felt like doing, which was punching something, maybe even Spencer.

'I know, I know, you've done a great job here,' Spencer said quickly. 'I heard you were awarded a Michelin star. Congratulations. How many restaurants do you have now?'

'Seven.'

'Amazing.'

Ben said nothing. He could feel his jaw bunch, his teeth grit. He didn't need Spencer's patronising praise.

'The thing is, you might have heard about the deal with The Harrington in the news…'

'That it didn't go through? Yeah, I might have heard that.' The two hotel empires had been all over the news lately, what with all the conflict over The Chatsfield's proposed buying out of The Harrington, and then his brother James's engagement to Leila, the princess of Surhaadi. James had proposed to Leila in front of The Chatsfield's hotel in New York, after first taking out a bill-board in Times Square declaring his love for her. The whole thing had become the kind of media circus Ben hated, but the public had lapped it up and The Chatsfield's popularity had soared.

'The Harringtons are going to have to come around at some point,' Ben told Spencer, his tone dismissive. 'They don't have as big an operation as The Chatsfield. They don't have the resources to withstand you.'

'The negotiations are going to be delicate,' Spencer answered. 'I have some of the sharehold-ers on board, but not all of them. Yet.'

Ben shrugged. He didn't care about either of the hotels, not any more.

'Look,' Spencer said. "I need to be on-site, in New York and London, dealing with this buy-out. It's at a critical stage just now, and I've got to be there.'

'So be there.'

'And I'm meant to be in Berlin starting next week, overseeing the hotel during the Berlinale.'

'The what?'

'The film festival.' Ben just stared, nonplussed, and Spencer continued. 'Most of the Hollywood types stay at The Chatsfield for the festival. It's an important time for the hotel, and for the com-pany as a whole.'

'I'm not sure why you're telling me all this,'

Ben told him, even though he was starting to have a suspicion.

'I need someone on-site,' Spencer explained. 'A Chatsfield.'

And he was a Chatsfield. 'So you expect me to drop my own business, my whole life, and head over to Berlin to help you out?' Ben filled in, his voice dripping disbelief. 'And all this after fourteen years of silence?'

Spencer's eyes flashed with sudden temper. 'You're the one who left, Ben.'

Ben nearly took a swing then. He felt his hands bunch into fists and his heart start to race. The desire to hit Spencer felt almost overwhelming, but he choked it down, as he always did. Once his anger had left a man nearly dead. Now he forced himself to breathe evenly, to relax his clenched fists.

'So I did. And I'm not coming back for you or your hotel, Spencer.'

Spencer's gaze flicked over him. 'You've changed,' he said quietly.

'Yes.'

'But you're still my brother, Ben,' Spencer continued with a small, sad smile. 'And I'm still yours. Maybe I should have got in touch before now. Hell, I know I should have. But you could have too. We're both to blame, aren't we?'

The old Ben would have tripped over himself

to accept the blame, to apologise, to make it right. To do whatever it took to make Spencer happy, his whole family dancing a damned jig. This Ben, the man who had had fourteen years of work-focused isolation and suppressed bitterness and rage, just shrugged.

'Please,' Spencer said. He tilted his head to one side, gave Ben the whimsical, lopsided smile he remembered so well from their childhood, a smile that felt as if it catapulted him back in time, back to the boy he'd once been. 'I need you, Ben.'

Still Ben shook his head, resisted that tug towards the past. 'I just opened a restaurant in Rome that I was planning on visiting...'

'Two weeks, Ben, that's all. We need to be a family again in this, stand united behind The Chatsfield. I want that more than anything.'

A united family. That was all he'd wanted when he'd been a kid. He'd suffered his parents' arguments, his father's rage, and had tried over and over again to make it all better. He'd sacrificed himself on the altar of his family once already, and here he was coming back for more. Because he knew then that he was going to agree. He'd regretted leaving all those years ago, even though it had felt like the only choice he could make. Regretted being the one to tear their family apart, and now he wondered if he could actually make amends. Make things better.

Ever the peacemaker.

'Two weeks,' he said neutrally, and relief broke over his brother's face like sunlight.

'Yes…'

'I'm a chef, not a front-of-house man. I leave all that to other people.'

'You'll be fine,' Spencer assured him. 'It's just a lot of smiling and handholding, honestly.'

Right. Ben shook his head, still wanting to refuse, knowing he wouldn't. Knowing he hadn't changed as much as he thought he had. He was just angry about it now.

'I haven't had anything to do with The Chatsfield for fourteen years,' he reminded Spencer. Reminded himself. 'Nearly half of my life.'

'All the more reason to come back to it now,' Spencer told him, and Ben heard the throb of sincerity in his brother's voice. 'I've missed you, Ben. I'm sorry you ran away all those years ago. I know you were trying to protect me…'

'Forget it.' Ben felt his throat close up, although whether from anger or grief or just pure, nameless emotion he couldn't say. He didn't want to talk about the past. He didn't even want to think about it.

'I appreciate what you were trying to do,' Spencer insisted, and Ben cut him off with a quick shake of his head. He really didn't want to talk about this.

When he finally trusted himself to speak, he said, 'Fine. I'll deal with the Berlin hotel for you. But I want something in return.' His brother wouldn't get his unquestioned loyalty any more. Things had changed too much for that. He'd changed.

Spencer raised his eyebrows, waiting. 'Okay. What do you want?'

'I want you to open a branch of my bistro in The Chatsfield, London.'

Spencer blinked, started shaking his head. 'London already has a Michelin-starred restaurant…'

'And the chef is about to retire. He's been losing his touch for years anyway.' Ben raised his eyebrows in cool challenge. 'So?'

Spencer stared at him for a long moment, and Ben stared back. Tension simmered in the air between them, tension and resentment that was decades old that neither of them had ever acknowledged.

Finally Spencer nodded. 'Fine. Oversee the film festival and I'll look into opening your restaurant in London.'

'More than just look into it,' Ben replied evenly. 'I want a signed contract.'

Spencer arched an eyebrow, gave a small smile. 'Don't you trust me?'

'This is business.'

'Fine.' Spencer nodded his assent. 'Send something to my office and I'll sign it. Now are we good?'

Ben nodded slowly. 'Yeah, we're good.'

Spencer let out a laugh as he shook his head. 'You drive a hard bargain, Ben. You've toughened up since I last saw you.'

When he'd been eighteen and utterly naive? Yeah, he'd changed just a little. But for the first time it really hit Ben that Spencer was here, that his family had, at least in part, been restored to him, and through the anger he felt something else, something clean and cool and welcome. Happiness.

CHAPTER ONE

OLIVIA HARRINGTON STARED at the standard room she'd booked at The Chatsfield and suppressed a groan. She'd seen broom cupboards that were bigger. By a lot.

Letting out a weary sigh, she kicked off the heels she'd worn for her red-eye flight from LA, and let go of her suitcase before sinking onto the edge of the narrow bed. Reaching one foot out, she swung the door shut and stared again at the prison cell she was supposed to call her home for the next week or so.

All right, she hadn't been expecting the Presidential Suite. She wasn't an A-lister by any means, but she was here for the film festival and a standard room at the best hotel in town surely meant more than this tiny closet? She didn't even have an en-suite bathroom, and the window was facing a concrete wall that she could reach out and touch if she were so inclined. She was not.

Plus it didn't look as if the room had been

cleaned properly since the last guest—or should she say inmate?—had stayed here. There were crumbs on the carpet and the bed covers were decidedly rumpled and, peering closer, she saw, stained.

Ugh.

With a gusty sigh she leaned forward and opened the door of the tiny fridge wedged under the tinier TV. This called for a drink.

Except the minibar had been raided by some former disgruntled or desperate guest; the only thing left in it was a bottle of water and an already opened bar of chocolate with two bites missing. Olivia stared at the chilled expanse of emptiness in disbelief. Could today get any worse?

She'd had two flights cancelled from LA, had been wedged into an economy seat with a mother with a screaming baby on one side and an officious businessman who hogged the armrest on the other. She'd been dressed to impress, knowing the paparazzi loved taking photos of stars without make-up as they stumbled off a plane, and her feet had been killing her now for a good thirteen hours. Sleep was a distant memory.

And this pathetic excuse for a hotel room was the last straw. Fired by indignation, Olivia rose from the bed, jammed her aching feet back into her heels and refreshed her lipstick, squinting into the tiny square of mirror above the bureau. She was *not* a diva, but this was ridiculous. She could barely breathe in a room this size, much less get ready for film premieres and networking parties. And she knew exactly why she had been given a broom cupboard.

Because she was a Harrington. Because her sister Isabelle had refused Spencer Chatsfield's offer to buy her shares in The Harrington, and let the Chatsfields swoop in and take over their family business. And mostly, she suspected, because Spencer Chatsfield thought it would be amusing to see a Harrington crammed into a Chatsfield cupboard.

Ha bloody ha ha.

All right, maybe she shouldn't have booked into The Chatsfield, knowing the current tension between the two families. But everyone who was everyone at the Berlin Film Festival stayed at The Chatsfield, and Olivia wasn't about to miss out simply because of family pride. She had too much riding on this festival, had worked too hard for too long to lose the first chance she'd had of actually proving herself simply because she wasn't staying at the right hotel. She knew how these things worked. It was all schmooze, schmooze, schmooze, and kiss, kiss, kiss. Networking. And she needed to do it. She'd do just about anything to secure her film career. To prove she'd made the right decision, sinking everything she had and was into being an actress. To honour her mother's memory, and make her proud.

Besides, Isabelle was the one who couldn't say the name Chatsfield without spitting; Olivia had never been that involved with the family business or its competitors.

But damned if she was going to sit by and let anyone, especially a Chatsfield, walk all over her.

With one last determined glance at her reflection, she wrenched open the door of her hotel room and stormed out, slamming it satisfyingly behind her as she went in search of the man who had thought it would be amusing to see a Harrington brought low.

Downstairs in the lobby of the hotel, actors, actresses and media types swarmed the lobby, all soaring gilt and marble and art nouveau glamour. Olivia saw a few people she knew, and she worked her way across the room, air-kissing and finger-waggling with the best of them, before she finally reached the concierge desk.

'I'd like to speak to the manager, please.'

The coiffed woman at the desk raised elegant eyebrows in polite incredulity. 'I'm afraid Mr Chatsfield is busy, Miss…?'

'Harrington. Olivia Harrington.' The receptionist looked decidedly unimpressed, and Olivia gritted her teeth. Okay, so she wasn't recognisable. Yet. But she had a supporting role in one of the films being shown this week, and the promise of an even bigger role in a film she really cared about, the kind of film that would touch hearts and win awards. She didn't need this receptionist to know who she was, but she did need her to cooperate.

'I'm sure Mr Chatsfield is busy,' she told the woman with honeyed sweetness, 'but considering I'm a Harrington, of the Harrington Hotel, I think he'll see me, don't you?'

Uncertainty wavered across the woman's face and Olivia leaned forward, still smiling. 'Trust me on this one,' she said.

Irritation chased after uncertainty on the woman's face, but with one tight nod she turned from the desk. 'I'll see if Mr Chatsfield is available,' she said, and Olivia nodded back, blowing out a breath of relief even as tension coiled more tightly inside her. First hurdle passed. Too bad there were only about a gazillion more.

'Olivia Harrington?'

Ben stared blankly at the receptionist standing in the doorway of his office behind the lobby area. He had a million and two problems to deal with, namely a truckload of A-list celebrities who thought requests like a magnum of pink champagne and fresh flowers—but no lilies or roses—in every room of their suites were reasonable.

He'd already had half a dozen bouquets sent back down because each one contained a rose. Singular.

Ben had been more than ready to tell the self-important starlet just where she could put all those flowers. Fortunately he'd managed to restrain himself, if only just. But when he next saw Spencer he was going to tell him where he could put the flowers. His brother had told him it would be a lot of handholding, but the level of attention these Hollywood types needed was unbelievable. And being back at The Chatsfield—any Chatsfield—with all of the memories and anger and pain—made him even less willing to deal with these outrageous requests. There was a reason he stayed in the kitchen.

Now he eyed the receptionist wearily, managing to remember her name after a few endless seconds. "You mean a Harrington, of *The* Harrington, is asking to see me, Anna?'

Anna nodded. 'She requested to see the manager. She was quite…forceful.'

Ben closed his eyes briefly. Perfect. A forceful Harrington who wanted to see him. What the hell was a Harrington doing in Berlin? Weren't all of these *delicate negotiations* meant to be taking place in London and New York?

'Thank you,' he said, forcing a smile for the receptionist. 'Send her in.'

* * *

The receptionist kept Olivia waiting for ten excruciating minutes—those stupid heels really hurt—before she finally returned with an icy smile.

'Mr Chatsfield will see you, Miss Harrington,' she said, her eyes like flint. 'Please come this way.'

'Thank you,' Olivia answered, unable to keep an edge of sarcasm from creeping into her voice. Wasn't The Chatsfield supposed to be number one in customer service? If this woman's behaviour was anything to go by, not to mention her shabby room, Olivia didn't think much of the luxury hotel's treatment of guests. But then, she was a Harrington. Maybe they reserved the rudeness and squalor especially for her.

With that unpleasant thought in the forefront of her mind, she followed the receptionist into an office behind the lobby, and stared at the man who sat behind the desk, one hand driven carelessly through his messy brown hair.

Was this Spencer Chatsfield? Olivia hadn't remembered from the few tabloid photographs she'd seen of him that he was quite so…*hot*. Wasn't Spencer buttoned-up and corporate-looking? The man in front of her was anything but. All right, yes, he was wearing a suit. A very nice suit in grey pinstripe, but he had the kind of body, the kind of attitude, that made him seem as if he'd be more at home in worn jeans and a faded T-shirt, maybe a leather motorcycle jacket. Yes, she could totally see that.

And way too late Olivia realised she was staring. Maybe even ogling. She drew herself up, kept her chin tilted high. Time to play the icily outraged guest.

'Spencer Chatsfield?' she said, her voice cool and clipped, and the man in front of her—he had stubble, she saw, glinting on his jaw…so, *so* sexy—arched an eyebrow.

'No. Ben Chatsfield. And you are?'

'Olivia Harrington.'

His eyes narrowed, his expression not even bordering on courteous. He looked…bored. 'And what can I do for you, Miss Harrington?' he asked in a voice that came close to a drawl.

He knew about the room, Olivia thought. She could see it in his hazel eyes, narrowed so knowingly, the way he lounged in his chair seeming relaxed yet emanating a barely leashed energy. He so knew.

She hadn't been aware of Ben Chatsfield's existence before a few seconds ago—Spencer was the one Isabelle had mentioned the most, and of course James was in the news—but Olivia knew one thing already. Ben Chatsfield was an ass.

She planted her hands on the desk and thrust her face towards his, deliberately invading his personal space. Ben Chatsfield didn't so much as flicker an eyelid.

'You may think it's amusing,' she said in a steely voice, 'to put a Harrington in a room that resembles a broom cupboard, but I happen to think it's poor customer service. *Very* poor customer service, Mr Chatsfield, and as I am a paying customer, I don't think highly of you or your hotel. At all.' She was huffing a bit by the end of this little speech, and Ben Chatsfield hadn't even changed expression.

'Am I to take it,' he asked after a long beat, 'that you're not satisfied with your hotel room?'

Olivia let out a rather inelegant laugh of disbelief. 'Yes, you are to *take* it, Mr Chatsfield. My room is completely appalling.'

'Appalling,' he repeated neutrally. He'd leaned back in his chair, his thumb and forefinger flexed to brace the side of his face, his eyes still narrowed.

Why, Olivia wondered in irritation, did he have to be so darned sexy? She straightened, folding her arms, waiting for him to—what? Justify his behaviour? Pretend that giving her that wretched room had been some sort of oversight?

As if.

'And what,' Ben asked in a voice of deliberate, and likely deceptive, mildness, 'is so *appalling* about your room…Miss Harrington?'

She simply gaped at him for a moment, utterly amazed by the sheer gall of him. 'Everything,' she finally said, glaring at him. 'Absolutely everything.'

In one quick and fluid move of powerful grace Ben leaned forward and started clicking away at his computer. Olivia waited, her temper barely held in check.

'I see from your reservation that you have booked a standard room.'

'Nothing,' she told him through gritted teeth, 'is standard about the broom cupboard I'm currently in.'

'The Chatsfield,' he told her coolly, 'does not run to broom cupboard.'

'Then maybe you should have a look at my room.'

He stared at her for a moment, his eyes still narrowed, his mouth thinned. And now that she was looking at his lips, Olivia had to admit they were sexy too. Surprisingly full and mobile and, well, lush. Lush lips on a very masculine man. He had long eyelashes too, she noticed. So unfair.

'Perhaps you're right. I *should* see this appalling room for myself,' he told her, his voice edged with sarcasm, 'and address any concerns you have.'

Olivia threw an arm out to gesture towards the door. 'Be my guest.'

'Ah,' Ben answered as he rose from behind his desk. 'Now that's my line.'

So a Harrington heiress decided to make a stink about her room. Suppressing a stab of irritation, Ben wondered just what had put Olivia's nose out of joint. Thread count not high enough on the sheets? No flowers in the bathroom? As much as he would have relished telling her to suck it up and deal, Ben knew he wouldn't. Or at least he'd do it nicely.

He turned back to Olivia, who was still looking at him with such obvious outrage that he almost wanted to roll his eyes. She was definitely putting it on a little thick, and for what? To amuse herself that she could stick it to a Chatsfield?

This wasn't his fight, he reminded himself. He might have agreed to help Spencer out, because…well, because his feelings for his family were complicated. But he didn't care about The Harrington, or whether The Chatsfield swallowed it whole or not. He certainly didn't care about this spoilt heiress.

'Would you care to show me your room?' he asked, his voice coolly polite, and with another huff she flounced past him and out into the lobby.

She was a beautiful woman, he had to acknowledge, although it was the kind of shiny, polished beauty that made him cynical. Too manufactured.

Too fake. And after all the lies he'd swallowed in his past, he didn't like fake anything.

Still, shiny, brown hair in carefully tousled locks that reached to the middle of her back. Big brown eyes. A dynamite figure, all willowy grace, encased in a jewel-green shift dress and high heels that drew Ben's reluctant admiration to her long, trim legs, and the tempting curve of her calves.

He yanked his gaze upwards and it fell on her butt. That was nice too. Up again, and he finally made contact with her shoulder blades as she marched ahead of him. Good. He'd keep his eyes trained there.

She stabbed the button for the lift with one French manicured fingernail, her body quivering with tension as they waited for it to arrive.

'When did you arrive in Berlin?' he asked, deciding solicitude was his best bet. Not that anything would impress this kind of high-maintenance woman, but at least he would have tried.

She turned to give him an icy stare. 'About an hour ago. I've been flying all night, Mr Chatsfield.'

And that was his problem how? Ben gave her a smile of bland equanimity. At least he hoped it was, and not the sneer he felt in his soul. 'Please, call me Ben.'

She didn't respond.

Thankfully the lift arrived and they stepped inside. At the last second before the doors closed a blowsy blonde woman in a bright pink designer tracksuit and sparkly high-tops squeezed in. She gave an obviously fake double take as she registered Olivia.

'*Olivia.* I didn't know you were coming to the festival.' Insincerity dripped from the woman's words and next to him Ben felt Olivia Harrington stiffen. After only a second she forced herself to relax, gave the woman what looked like a genuine smile but Ben knew in his gut was false.

'Amber. So nice to see you. Yes, I'm here. I have a role in *Blue Skies Forever.* The indie film?'

'Oh, right.' The woman, this Amber wrinkled her nose. 'A walk-on part?'

'A supporting role,' Olivia corrected, her smile not slipping so much as a millimetre. The lift doors pinged and she stepped past Amber her head held high. 'See you around, I'm sure.'

So she was an actress. Ben eyed her thoughtfully as she walked down the thickly carpeted hall, her chin lifted defiantly, her shoulders thrown back. It didn't really surprise him, he decided. She certainly had a flare for the dramatic. And actresses, he acknowledged, tended to be high maintenance, difficult and fake. Olivia had already shown she was all three. No, he wasn't surprised at all.

She took him down another hall, this one narrower than the hotel's main corridors, and then through a fire door that had Ben frowning. He didn't think there were any guest bedrooms in this part of the building. It was staff accommodation and storage.

'Here we are,' she announced sunnily, and with a deliberate flourish she produced her old-fashioned key—not one of the hotel's signature key cards—and unlocked the door to her room. Ben stepped inside, his shoulder brushing Olivia's because the room was that small.

It really was a broom cupboard. Or close enough to one.

'Would you call this appalling?' she asked with acid sweetness. She pointed to the rumpled, stained bed. 'I don't think the sheets have been changed in, oh, maybe a year? Plus the minibar has been raided, and there's no en-suite bathroom despite the fact that The Chatsfield's standard rooms are all meant to have them.' She whirled around to face him, her hands on her hips, her body, and in particular her breasts, quite close to his own anatomy. The room was *small*.

Ben held his ground, conscious of the way her hair had brushed his cheek when she'd whirled around, and how even after a thirteen-hour flight she smelled like strawberries. And vanilla.

He took a deep breath, kept his voice even and

his gaze on her furious face. 'I'm sorry. Clearly there's been a mistake.'

'A *mistake*? You're going to pretend putting me in this—this *sty* was a mistake?'

Fury, all too familiar a feeling, spiked. All right, she was pretty, but what was her problem? She seemed determined to get the most mileage out of what clearly had to be an accident.

'Yes, a mistake,' he answered, all solicitude gone from his voice. 'You don't actually think someone would intentionally put a guest in a room like this?'

She planted her hands on her hips, her eyes narrowed to chocolate-brown slits. 'That's exactly what I think, *Ben.*'

He stared at her, first incredulous, then scornful. 'You think I put you in this room because you're a Harrington?'

'It doesn't take a rocket scientist to figure that out.'

Ben let out one short, sharp laugh. 'You're no rocket scientist, sweetheart.'

Temper flashed in her eyes, turning them almost to gold. 'Don't patronise me…'

'I could say the same. You must think you're pretty damn important, for me to waste my time irritating you.'

She shrugged defiantly. 'If the shoe fits…'

'So you think I trawled through the guest list

during the film festival,' he cut her off, his voice dripping disbelief, 'when the hotel is completely booked, hoping that a Harrington *might* have made a reservation, just so I could make this petty power play?' He thought of the sugar-laced venom of the woman in the lift. 'Because, sorry to break it to you, Miss Harrington, but your presence in Berlin hasn't been plastered all over the news.' He raised his eyebrows, curved his mouth into a mocking smile. 'Actually, I'm not sure if the media have even twigged you're here.'

Fury blazed colour onto each high, lovely cheekbone and her eyes narrowed further. 'I don't know how you found out, but…'

'Oh, give it a rest.' He was so tired of prima donnas and their outrageous demands. The last thing he needed was a Harrington breathing down his neck. 'It was an honest mistake, and that's all. I didn't even know a Harrington was in Berlin. I assumed your whole family was in New York, working on the negotiations with my brother.'

'What negotiations?' Olivia demanded sharply. 'My sister refused…'

'I don't think corporate takeovers are quite that simple,' Ben answered dryly. 'But honestly, it has nothing to do with me. I have nothing to do with The Chatsfield.'

Olivia arched an incredulous eyebrow. 'Yet you're managing The Chatsfield, Berlin.'

Something that he still couldn't quite believe he'd agreed to. Didn't want to think about why he had. 'So I am,' he responded, his voice as even as he could make it. 'But only for the duration of the festival.'

'So the Chatsfields are close,' Olivia observed, her gaze sweeping over him, and Ben tensed. Close? He'd thought so. Once.

'We're family,' he said now, his voice toneless. 'Just like the Harringtons.'

Olivia pursed her lips and they stared at each other, anger simmering, along with something else. Something Ben was reluctant to admit to but could easily name. Attraction.

Olivia Harrington, personality aside, was a lovely woman. A beautiful, vibrant, sexy woman. With her eyes sparkling with all that self-righteous indignation, her hair tousled about her flushed face, she looked both angry and turned on.

And maybe she was both.

Ben knew he was.

He shifted where he stood, conscious that now was a pretty inconvenient time to show evidence of that attraction.

'I'll arrange for you to be moved to a different room,' he said in a tone of finality. 'And as an apology for our error, you can have one night's stay free of charge.'

Olivia's eyes widened in surprise but then she gave a curt nod, as if she expected no less. Of course. 'Thank you,' she said with some grace, and rather grimly Ben nodded back. The sooner he was quit of this woman, the better.

'Any time,' he said, and turned to leave the room.

CHAPTER TWO

LESS THAN AN hour later Olivia stepped into one of the executive suites of The Chatsfield, Berlin, and felt her jaw drop. This was definitely *not* a standard room. Not even close.

A bellhop had already brought her suitcase into the foyer, and now Olivia closed the door before slowly walking around the soaring suite of rooms: foyer, living area, kitchen, bedroom and a huge bathroom with a sunken marble tub. Amazing. Just looking at that tub made her yearn to climb into it and soak in a sea of fragrant bubbles for about, oh, a lifetime.

And yet as amazing as it all was, a tiny sliver of uncertainty needled her. Not only was she getting a night free of charge, but she was staying in a suite that had to cost about a quadrillion more euros than the standard room she'd originally booked.

Was Ben Chatsfield just providing the kind of stellar customer service expected from The

Chatsfield, or was he feeling guilty because he really had put her in that broom cupboard on purpose?

She decided not to overthink it. Either way, she had a fabulous room and was spending less money than she'd budgeted, which was a good thing since she didn't use Harrington money to fund her life or her dreams.

She unpacked, hanging up her carefully co-ordinated outfits in the enormous wardrobe before running the huge tub she'd been fanta-sising about and loading it with half the bottle of complimentary bubble bath. She stripped off her clothes and slipped inside all that fragrant warmth. Bliss.

Yet even as she leaned her head back against the marble tub and closed her eyes, she felt that uncertainty needle her again. Although maybe it wasn't actually uncertainty. Maybe it was just… awareness.

Ben Chatsfield had no right to look that attrac-tive. That *hot*. With her eyes closed she could picture him perfectly: the slightly messed brown hair, the glinting hazel eyes, the strong, stubbled jaw. Gorgeous. But even more alluring than his good looks, Olivia decided, had been his energy. Raw and barely restrained. Wild. *Real*.

She laughed softly, because even if Ben Chats-field had ever been interested in her, she knew she wouldn't know what to do with a man like that. Her handful of relationships so far had been carefully controlled, stage-managed affairs that bore little resemblance to reality—or wildness.

She didn't even *want* wild. Or real. Any depth of emotion was anathema to her, and had been since she was twelve. She hadn't handled it then, and she couldn't handle it now. She chose not to, and had kept herself from anything intimate or emotional or real with anyone. She'd certainly keep herself from it with someone like Ben Chatsfield.

And yet as she slid deeper into the tub, she still wondered what he would be like if he gave in to that wildness and let his exterior slip just a little. What she would be like with him.

Sighing, she slid deeper into the water until the bubbles came right up to her nose. No point thinking about Ben Chatsfield, because nothing was going to happen there. She'd make sure of it. Tonight she'd wear comfy pyjamas and watch mindless rom-coms on the huge TV in the bedroom and then sleep for at least eight hours. Tomorrow she had a full day of interviews lined up for her upcoming film, and she'd have to be on the whole time. One huge twelve-hour performance, which was fine, because it was far easier to be Olivia Harrington, the up-and-coming actress, than anyone else. Like herself.

* * *

Ben gritted his teeth as the A-list actress pouted prettily at him. She was gorgeous, this woman whose name he'd forgotten, he'd give her that, but she was also irritating as hell. Almost as irritating as Olivia Harrington.

'I'm afraid the lobby is not able to be reserved,' he told the actress, his voice clipped, bordering on abrupt. Standing in the lobby of The Chatsfield was hard enough without having to kowtow to a rich bimbo. Memories assailed him everywhere he turned, and he'd never even been to Berlin before. But he'd been to The Chatsfield. As soon as he'd stepped through the lobby doors he'd felt as if he'd stumbled into a time machine. The clink of crystal, the smell of leather and furniture polish, the ping of the lifts…all of it had brought him right back to the boy he'd been, spit-shined and eager, waiting in the lobby for his father to be finished with work. Hoping that this time his father would smile at him. Smile at Spencer.

'But it would be the perfect venue for my birthday party,' the actress insisted, and Ben was brought back to the present, which was both a relief and an annoyance. She dropped the pout, offering him a sultry smile instead. It made for a change at least, as did the hand she laid on his arm. The woman didn't provoke even a quarter of the reaction Olivia Harrington had. 'Please?' she asked breathily, fluttering false eyelashes.

'The lobby is a public place,' Ben answered, and deliberately removed his arm from her hand. 'And other guests need to use it to access their rooms. Unless you don't mind having them all go through the service entrance?' He'd said it sarcastically enough, unable to help himself, but he could see the woman had taken him seriously. From behind her he saw a staff member smother a smile, and he was glad someone was enjoying this conversation. 'I'm sorry, but it's absolutely not possible,' he told the woman firmly. 'We would be happy to accommodate the needs of your event in any of The Chatsfield's reception rooms.' He took a step back, tilting his head to indicate the concierge desk. 'Shall I have someone show you the options? The Parisian Salon is particularly stunning.'

He grimaced as he turned away, hating the honey-eyed falseness that was starting to come to him all too easily. For fourteen years he'd thrived on a reputation of being honest to the point of bluntness. People knew what they were getting with Ben's Bistro. It was only stepping back into The Chatsfield, into the web of deceit his parents had woven since infancy, that he'd become a flatterer. Which was what Spencer had asked him to be.

'Nicely handled, Mr Chatsfield.' The bellhop

who had overheard his conversation came up to him with a grin. 'That woman was seriously annoying. She had *eight* pieces of luggage and she didn't even tip.'

'I'm not surprised,' Ben answered even though he knew a regular manager would have given the bellhop a smack-down for talking about guests that way. He wouldn't. He'd taken the measure of most of the staff within the first few days, and he knew he needed to draw a line between stellar customer service and surrendering your dignity. This bellhop had been nothing but courteous to all the guests. No wonder he needed to let off some steam.

He offered him a quick smile before he nodded towards the luggage trolleys and had the boy hurrying back to his place. Order still needed to be kept.

'Mr Chatsfield?' Heels clicked behind him and he turned to see his PA, Rebecca, smiling uncertainly at him.

'Rebecca. What can I do for you?'

'A reporter from the entertainment network wanted to interview you for their piece about catering to the stars?'

'Oh. Right.' And that was something he really felt like doing. Trying not to grimace, Ben followed Rebecca to the waiting reporter.

Twelve hours later, with it heading on to midnight, Ben was finally able to relax. He'd put out more fires—including an actual one when a guest had knocked over one of the two hundred aromatherapy candles she'd scattered around her suite—and soothed more giant egos than he cared to remember. And he hadn't lost his temper. He hadn't lost his temper in fourteen years, but he was holding on to it now by a thread. Tension knotted his shoulders and his head throbbed.

He shouldn't have come back to The Chatsfield, he acknowledged as he headed to the rooftop pool for a swim. He shouldn't have thought he could handle the memories, the emotions. Sighing, he stripped off his suit in the men's changing room and headed into the pool area.

The Chatsfield's swimming pool was one of the highlights of the hotel, an Olympic-size pool on the roof, glassed in on all sides, with a panoramic view of the city. Swimming laps had always been one way Ben liked to relax, to burn off the excess emotion and stress.

The pool was thankfully empty at this late hour, and Ben could see the city stretching out in every direction, sparkling under the night sky. He could make out the Bellevue Palace as well as the iconic Victory Column, and the dark expanse of the Tiergarten now covered in a thin dusting of snow. He'd never been to Berlin before now, and he didn't think he was going to have much time to see the sights during the two weeks he was here.

Not that he cared. He just wanted to get back to France. To his life.

And if Spencer asks you to open restaurants in all the Chatsfield hotels?

It was a question that had dogged Ben since he'd made the demand of his brother because the truth was he wasn't even sure he *wanted* to open restaurants in all of the hotels. He didn't need the money or the publicity, and the thought of linking himself so closely to The Chatsfields—and to the Chatsfield family—made his gut churn.

You couldn't go back. Ever. Even if you wanted to.

But did he want to?

Shoving the question aside, Ben dove into the pool. The water felt cool and refreshing and his head started to clear. The tension between his shoulder blades loosened and he did a couple of laps before flipping onto his back and staring up at the domed ceiling as he let his mind empty out.

A door squeaked open and Ben lifted his head from the water; he could only see a pair of trim ankles and curvy calves coming towards the pool. Someone had clearly had the same idea as he had.

He flipped back onto his stomach and started

to swim towards the edge. His fifteen minutes of relaxation were clearly over.

He was about a metre from the pool's side when he saw something in his peripheral vision, too late for him to do anything about it, and then he felt the breath leave his body in a rush as the female guest who had just entered the pool area dove straight into him.

Olivia felt as if she'd just dived into concrete. Stars danced through her dazed mind and she let out an undignified shriek, her head pounding from the impact, before arms clasped her shoulders like bands of iron.

'Do you *always*,' a familiar, masculine voice asked in disgust, 'leap before you look?'

Olivia blinked the water from her eyes and shook her wet hair from her face. And stared into the angry, arrogant face of Ben Chatsfield.

His eyes blazed and his cheeks were slashed with colour and for a moment, her mind still dazed, Olivia thought he looked like some ancient water god emerging from the sea, water dripping off his perfectly formed pecs.

Then sanity returned and she started to sputter.

'I didn't see anyone in the pool,' she said, and her sputtering erupted into a coughing fit. She'd swallowed several mouthfuls of pool water when she'd made contact with Ben Chatsfield's chest.

A chest that was now pressed alarmingly close to hers. Ben was still gripping her by the shoulders, their legs tangled together in the water. Her heart was thudding from the shock of the encounter, and something else as well.

Something she had no intention of acknowledging. In any case, she was coughing too much to say or even think anything.

Ben muttered something under his breath and with one arm under her armpits and across her breasts he started towing her to the side of the pool as if she were unconscious.

'Just a *second…*' she began, and started coughing again.

He hauled himself up onto the pool's ledge and then unceremoniously hauled her up next to him. She lay slumped against him, his arm around her shoulders, as she attempted to cough up a lung.

Thankfully her coughing finally subsided and she drew in several agonised but much needed breaths. 'Thank you,' she mumbled. 'I must have swallowed some pool water.'

'Must have,' Ben agreed tonelessly, and Olivia wondered why, out of all the people in the hotel, she had to dive straight into Ben Chatsfield.

She looked up at him, tried not to notice the water droplets that clung to his eyelashes and his chin…and his chest. Her gaze dropped down of its own accord and she swallowed hard at the sight of Ben Chatsfield's well-toned six-pack. Nice.

Okay, looking up again. She smiled weakly and Ben smiled back, a cold curving of his mouth that told her she was *so* busted. Well, fine. A girl could look.

'What did you mean, do I always leap before I look?' she demanded, his words coming back to her rather belatedly.

'Exactly that. You dived into a pool without checking if someone was swimming in it.'

'I didn't see you,' she snapped.

'Because you didn't look.'

All right, maybe she hadn't looked. She'd been tired and distracted and pretty darn grumpy because the first day of the festival had basically sucked. Two interviews cancelled, another reporter claiming she wasn't interesting enough because her role in the film that was going to be her big breakthrough wasn't yet confirmed, and she'd learned that twelve of her thirty-two lines had been cut from *Blue Skies Forever*, the indie film that was being shown at the festival.

And so she hadn't done all her Girl Scout safety checks before jumping into the pool. Whatever.

'I meant,' she asked Ben now, 'what you meant when you said *always*. As if you had experience of me jumping you in the pool before.' Too late she realised what she'd said. 'I mean, jumping *on* you.'

'I know what you meant,' Ben answered, and Olivia wanted to slap that knowing smirk right off his face. Or maybe kiss him. Both, probably, one after the other. Not good. Ben was out of her league, in a whole lot of ways.

She edged away from him and after a tiny pause Ben slipped his arm from her shoulders. She shivered, and then wished she hadn't.

'I said always,' Ben told her, 'because you pretty much leaped before you looked yesterday, when you came into my office with all your guns blazing, having made the assumption that I put you in that room on purpose.'

Olivia folded her arms across her chest. She had just remembered that she was wearing a skimpy hot-pink bikini. She'd forgotten to pack a normal swimsuit for exercise, because she'd been so focused on clothes she would be seen in. The wardrobe of a future Hollywood star.

'I think it was a fair assumption to make,' she told Ben coolly. 'In fact, I'm far from convinced that you didn't do it on purpose.'

Temper flared in Ben's eyes, quickly tamped down, but even angry, especially angry, he looked hot. 'Of course you are.'

'Now what is that supposed to mean?' she demanded, straightening in affront even as attraction jolted her insides in little lightning streaks. Ben slipped back into the pool, turning to face her with eyes that blazed and a mouth twisted downwards in derision.

'Just that you're exactly what you look and sound like, Miss Harrington. A high-maintenance, shallow, self-important wannabe celebrity. And so naturally you would think that the world revolves around you and your family, when in fact I couldn't care less about the Harringtons, much less which room one of them is put in, in a hotel I'm only managing for two weeks. Goodnight.'

And with her mouth hanging inelegantly open, Olivia could only stare as Ben swam away from her, his lithe body cutting quickly through the water. He hauled himself up on the other side of the pool and then strode into the men's changing room, slamming the door behind him.

All right, he should not have said all of that. Any of that. Yet it had felt good to let a little of his anger out, even if a lot of it wasn't directed at Olivia Harrington.

Ben closed his eyes as he stepped under the changing room's shower and let the hot spray hit him full in the face.

Maybe he'd been a little unfair.

And Olivia Harrington was just the type of person to create a huge fuss about how she'd been treated. She could go to the papers and create an enormous brouhaha about it. The media would have a field day.

Ben leaned his head against the marble tile and swore. What had he been thinking?

Well, he hadn't been thinking. He'd just been reacting—to the stress of his day and the nearness of Olivia Harrington, to the fact that he'd been able to see her nipples through the thin fabric of her bikini top, and to being back at The Chatsfield, struggling to keep from reverting to the boy he'd once been or the man he knew he really was.

All of it had made him speak without consulting his brain first. And while it had felt good at the time, he wasn't so keen on the possible repercussions.

He could, he supposed, apologise. He doubted it would do much good but he ought to at least make the effort. Sighing, he switched off the shower and wrapped a towel around his waist. He dressed quickly in the workout shorts and T-shirt he'd worn to the pool and then went back in search of Olivia.

Unfortunately, when he entered the pool area, it was empty. Olivia Harrington was gone.

Olivia sat shivering on the edge of the pool as Ben's words reverberated through her. Her mouth was still hanging open in shock. No one had ever talked to her like that before. Well, not since sixth grade, when she'd been bullied by a bunch of mean girls.

Not that a bit of name-calling had hurt her much back then. She'd been too focused on the far more consuming matter of her mother dying.

And as for now…well, sticks and stones, Olivia told herself firmly. Sticks and stones, that was all. She wasn't going to be hurt by Ben Chatsfield's scathing assessment of her, or the contempt she'd seen blazing in those hazel eyes.

And she wasn't self-important. Or shallow. As for high maintenance, well, she was an actress. She did have an appearance to maintain. And *wannabe*…well, that was just plain insulting.

Her expression hardening, and her mouth thankfully closing, Olivia scrambled up from the edge of the pool and stalked towards the women's changing room.

Okay, so maybe she'd overreacted a little about the room, she acknowledged as she showered and changed back into her clothes. But was she seriously meant to believe that it had been an accident? She doubted that such a tiny room was even on the reservation system. But Ben had given her a huge suite, and a night's free accommodation, so…

She could be the bigger person here. She'd apologise to him for her accusation, and then give him a chance to apologize for all those insults. Tomorrow morning she'd graciously accept his grovelling, Olivia decided. She was looking forward to Ben offering her a little bit of the legendary Chatsfield customer service.

Just six hours later Olivia was up and ready to go, dressed to kill or at least to impress in a lavender dress with a cinched-in waist and flared skirt. She left her hair artfully tousled around her shoulders, spent half an hour on her understated make-up and wore a single silver bangle on her wrist, as well as the silver heart pendant she never took off; her mother had given it to her just before she'd died. She looked professional but pretty, and ready, Olivia hoped, to nail a day full of interviews as well as Berlin's arctic February winds. She'd brought a matching coat, at any rate.

She managed to choke down some fruit and coffee—she forewent the traditional German breakfast of cold meats—and then went in search of Ben before she headed out for her first interview. It was just a little past seven in the morning, but Ben was already at his desk, already looking deliciously rumpled, one hand driven carelessly through his hair.

Olivia experienced a little pulse of attraction and squashed it firmly. She was going to apologise like the professional, non-shallow person she was, and then she was going to graciously accept his apology, and *then* she was going to move on and never think about Ben Chatsfield again.

'Hello.'

He looked up from his computer, his hazel eyes narrowing to glints of grey-green as he registered her presence. 'Please tell me there isn't a problem with your suite.'

'No, it's completely amazing actually.' She paused, unsure how to have an at least somewhat normal conversation with this man. He sat very still, but she still sensed that barely leashed energy and emotion emanating from him, and wondered at it. Okay, *normal* conversation. 'I can't believe that suite was available. I was under the impression that all the rooms were booked.'

Ben pressed his lips together and glanced back at his computer screen. 'Not that one.'

Olivia straightened, gave him her well-practised I'd-like-to-thank-the-Academy smile. 'Well, I came here to thank you, really, for letting me stay in it. I appreciate the effort you must have gone to, and I'm sorry for jumping to conclusions about why I had my original room. So thank you for addressing my concern.' She kept smiling as she waited for his reciprocal apology.

Ben's gaze flicked back to her for a millisecond. 'You're welcome.' Olivia stared. That was it? No apologies for calling her shallow and self-important and *wannabe*? 'I looked into the room confusion,' he continued without taking his gaze from the computer screen, 'and it seems that one of our newer reception staff gave your original room away to a rather intimidating guest. He put you in that room, thinking it had already been renovated. That wing of the hotel is undergoing renovations, but as you could see, they haven't finished yet.'

'Ah. Right.' And that did seem like a believable excuse, Olivia supposed. So yes, she *had* over-reacted. But so had he. Yet he obviously didn't feel the need to apologise for his litany of insults last night.

And then, just when she was ready to consign Ben to permanent jerkdom, he said abruptly, one hand curling into a fist on top of his desk, 'I'm sorry for losing my temper last night. It shouldn't have happened. I certainly shouldn't have insulted you. Please accept my apology.' Each word was bitten out, and his expression was unaccountably grim. Olivia watched as he carefully, deliberately, unclenched his fist, palm flat against the desk.

'Apology accepted.' She managed a teasing smile. 'Although that wannabe comment was completely uncalled for.'

To her surprise his mouth kicked up in a tiny, answering smile and the tension that had been keeping him so still seemed to flow out of him, at least a little. 'I thought that might annoy you the most.'

'Well spotted.'

'I am sorry.'

'Uh-huh.' Were they actually flirting? It kind of felt like it, which was…weird. But also rather stimulating. 'Just out of curiosity,' she asked, 'why *did* you have one of the largest suites in the hotel empty? I thought the hotel was fully booked. You didn't kick anyone out on my account, did you?'

He hesitated, then said, 'No.'

'So it was empty?'

'Not exactly.'

'Why do I feel like you're not telling me something?'

He shrugged and then admitted tersely, 'I was staying there.'

'*You* were?' Shock scorched through her, followed by a horrified remorse. She'd kicked Ben Chatsfield out of his room. 'Where are you staying now?'

His sardonic gaze met hers. 'Guess.'

The penny dropped with a clunk. 'Not…'

'I had the sheets changed, at least. But the hotel, as you noted yourself, is fully booked.'

She simply stared, utterly discomfited by his admission. *He* was staying in the broom cupboard? And he hadn't even been going to mention it until she'd pressed. Now she really did feel self-important and high maintenance and all the rest of it, except wannabe, of course 'Thank you,' she said yet again, lamely, and Ben just stared at her with that inscrutable expression, his eyes reminding her of a tiger or a panther or some other wild and dangerous animal. Okay, enough with the fanciful thoughts. He was waiting, she realised, for her to go. And so she did, hightailing it out of his office with an unsettling mixture of relief and disappointment.

An hour later Olivia had managed, mostly, to put the whole episode with Ben Chatsfield out of her mind as she answered questions about the upcoming drama that was going to be her ticket to the A-list. She laughed, she chatted, she even winked once. All of it a performance, and one that she was doing remarkably well, if she did say so herself.

Then, just after she'd told a witty joke and let out a sparkling laugh, a reporter came back with, 'Would you care to comment on your relationship with Benjamin Chatsfield?'

What the what?

The expression of laughing ease dropped from Olivia's face like the mask it was as she stared at the woman from the entertainment website with whom she'd got on very well until this moment.

Her relationship with Benjamin Chatsfield? How on earth had the woman come up with that one? After an endless moment her brain finally stuttered into gear. 'I don't care to comment at this time,' she said crisply. And wasn't *that* an understatement. She didn't have a relationship with Ben Chatsfield. How did this woman even know she'd *spoken* to Ben Chatsfield?

'Not even on this photo?' the woman asked with a smile that was starting to look smug. Olivia looked down at the newspaper she'd laid on the table, opened to a two-page spread of...

Oh, dear heaven.

How had someone seen them? And how had they looked so...*intimate*? Some paparazzi had captured them at just the right—or wrong—moment, with Ben's hands on her shoulders, his face thrust close to hers, looking for all the world as if he were going to kiss her when in fact he'd been about to yell at her. Again.

And there were other photos...one of them sitting by the edge of the pool, Ben's arm around her shoulders. She'd been recovering from a coughing fit but it looked...it looked as if they were cuddling.

And then the headline: *Celebrity Chef Ben Chatsfield Gets Up Close and Personal with Starlet.*

Starlet? They didn't even know her name! She swallowed her pique and glanced back up at the smirking woman.

'Like I said, no comment.'

Every interview she'd had scheduled that day was the same. Each reporter asked a few hurried questions about the upcoming film or her career, and then went for what they were really interested in.

Her relationship with *celebrity chef* Ben Chatsfield. Starlet she might be, but she'd been recognised.

Olivia kept up the 'no comment' line for five interviews, enduring smirks, chuckles and some pretty blatant innuendo. By late afternoon, when a jowly man from a tabloid her agent had insisted she grant an interview to asked her what she thought Ben Chatsfield saw in her, an insulting question if she'd ever heard one, she replied frostily, 'The truth is Ben Chatsfield and I have been seeing each other since The Chatsfield tried to take over The Harrington.' She gave him a glittering smile. 'It's a bit like *Romeo and Juliet*, don't you think?'

And without waiting for a response, she stalked out of the room.

Her agent, Melissa, followed her with a click of stiletto heels. 'Now that will get them talking,' she said with satisfaction. 'I didn't know you were seeing Ben Chatsfield. That's great press.'

Olivia kept her back to Melissa, unsure of the expression that would be on her face. Horror, probably. Or maybe hysteria. 'I'm not,' she said after a moment, her voice toneless.

'What was that?'

'I'm not seeing him!' She whirled around, gave her agent what she hoped was an insouciant look. *Come on, Olivia, play the devil-may-care ingénue. It's just another role.* 'I just said that because the man was so odious.'

'Oh.' Melissa frowned, and Olivia let out a careless little laugh.

'What? It's just Hollywood gossip. Tomorrow they'll move on to something else.'

'Yes, but…' Melissa was still frowning, and everything in Olivia prickled with annoyance—as well as a little alarm. She didn't like seeing her agent look so…disapproving.

'It's not a big deal,' she said, still trying for airy.

'You just confirmed a relationship,' Melissa pointed out. 'So it's not just gossip or rumour, Olivia. It's a fact, confirmed by a primary source.'

'Oh. Well.' Her mind raced even as her face flushed. *Why* had she said such a stupid thing? She'd just been so fed up, being treated like Ben Chatsfield's eye candy all day instead of an actress in her own right. No one had been interested in her upcoming film, just who they thought Ben Chatsfield was seeing. 'I could explain,' she suggested to Melissa. 'Tell them I just said it because that reporter was so annoying…' She trailed off as Melissa shook her head.

'That would just make you look like an idiot. An unstable idiot who lies in public.'

Which basically meant she *was* an unstable idiot who lied in public. Ben Chatsfield's mocking question echoed through her mind.

Do you always leap before you look?

Apparently so. Which was surprising, because she'd never thought of herself as impetuous. She'd planned her acting career with the resolute focus of a military general. Yet in the space of twenty-four hours she'd been acting like a crazed person. She was just so stressed. Isabelle was on her case about wanting to buy her shares in the hotel, and while Olivia had no real ties to the hotel, she still felt reluctant to step away from her family's business so completely. Her real focus, though, was on securing this film role which could make—or break—her career. She had not, Olivia acknowledged, been at her best.

No wonder Ben thought so little of her. And he was going to think even less of her when he heard about this latest mishap. Which he most certainly would, since she'd just said it to a voracious reporter.

This was bad.

'I screwed up, clearly,' she told Melissa. Honesty was the best policy, right? 'What can I do to make it better?'

'I'm not sure. What *is* your relationship with Ben Chatsfield, Olivia?'

'I told you, I don't have one...'

'Then why were the two of you in a clinch in The Chatsfield's pool?'

'It was an accident.'

'An *accident*?'

Olivia sighed. 'I didn't look before I leaped,' she said. 'Literally.'

At least Melissa gave a small smile when Olivia explained just how she and Ben had ended up tangled together in the deep end. But then she sighed and frowned again.

'I think the best thing, for now anyway, is to go along with the ruse.'

'The ruse?'

'That you're seeing Ben Chatsfield. Assuming you can get him to agree, of course.'

'Oh. Uh. Sure.' Not.

'At least until the Berlinale is over and we have this film role confirmed. After that you can just say the two of you broke up.'

'Right.' Ben was so not going to be on board with this. Olivia pictured the look of disbelief on his face when she explained what she wanted—needed—him to do. Not just disbelief, but disdain. Derision. All those nasty *D* words.

'So you guys are friends, right?' Melissa asked. 'He'll agree to play along for a little while?'

Olivia gave her agent a breezy smile. She wasn't an actress for nothing. 'Oh, sure,' she said, and held up two crossed fingers. 'We're like that. Not a problem at all.'

Uh-huh.

CHAPTER THREE

'HAVE YOU *SEEN* the newspapers?'

Ben held his cell phone away from his ear as Spencer's voice boomed down the line. 'The newspapers? No. I've been too busy trying to find proper accommodation for an actress's toy poodle. And by toy poodle, I don't mean toy. I mean a real-live dog she decided to bring with her to the hotel.'

'We have an arrangement with a local kennel,' Spencer said dismissively, and Ben gritted his teeth.

'That might have been good to know for the past two hours.' He drummed his fingers on the desk, forced his voice back to measured. 'So what's in the newspapers?'

'You are.'

'What?' Though he knew the media had dubbed him a celebrity chef, he'd managed to keep a low profile ever since he'd opened his first restaurant. He didn't want or need publicity; food spoke for itself. And he wasn't exactly the world's most charming people-person. He had no idea why he'd make the papers now.

'You and a certain Harrington,' Spencer elaborated, and for a second Ben still came up blank. 'A certain... You mean Olivia?' What other Harrington had he come into contact with, ever?

'Olivia, yes,' Spencer bit out. 'So when were you going to enlighten me that you're dating a Harrington?'

'I'm what?' Now Ben was the one booming. His PA, Rebecca, in the office adjoining his gave him a quick, curious glance. Ben sat back in his chair, drove one hand through his hair and let out a low breath.

'I am not dating a Harrington. Any Harrington, and definitely not Olivia. Not,' he continued with a definite edge to his voice, 'that I need to answer to you if I was.'

'So you are...'

'No. I'm just reminding you that I'm not your damn employee, Spencer. I'm doing you a favour for two weeks, and my personal life is none of your concern.'

Spencer was silent for a moment. 'Fair enough,' he said at last, and he sounded grudging. 'But the newspapers are saying you are dating a Harrington, and that affects the negotiations...'

'Then the newspapers are wrong,' Ben answered shortly. 'What a surprise.'

'That's not what Olivia is saying,' Spencer added, and Ben bolted upright, his hand clenched so tightly around his phone his knuckles ached.

'What?'

'She gave an interview this afternoon, which is breaking news on all the entertainment websites as we speak. I quote, "We've been seeing each other since The Chatsfield tried to take over The Harrington." And the *we* in that, in case you're wondering, is you and Olivia.'

Ben's jaw went slack as his mind spun. So this was her revenge for his smack-down last night? So much for the heartfelt apology she'd given him that morning. Clearly she had more acting talent than he'd given her credit for.

Instead she decided to tell the worldwide media that they were *dating*?

What the hell was that about? Was she trying to embarrass or annoy him, or both?

Well, he was definitely annoyed. Infuriated, actually, and he took a deep breath to control the rush of anger he felt, justified as it was.

'I have no idea why she would say that,' he told Spencer. 'I barely know the woman.'

'Barely?' Spencer repeated, sounding more than a little sceptical.

'Yes, barely,' Ben snapped. 'And I don't appreciate the inquisition. I met her when she stormed down here accusing me of putting her in a sub-standard room on purpose, because she was a Harrington.'

'Did you?'

Ben rose from his chair at that, pacing the room to release some of the energy boiling inside him. 'What do you think?' he demanded. 'I've told you before—I have zero interest in your deal with The Harrington. I couldn't care less, Spencer, what the hell you do with your hotel. So no, I didn't put some woman I didn't even know in a small room as some kind of petty revenge. And that's the last I'm going to say on it.' He stopped, breathing hard, his hand clenching the phone so tightly his knuckles ached.

'I'm sorry,' Spencer said quietly, and Ben had the unsettling sense that Spencer was apologising for something else, that this conversation, at least from his end, had been about more than Olivia Harrington.

He sank back into his chair, took a few even breaths. Spencer let out a weary sigh. 'It's just been one hot mess after another with this whole deal. And now the negotiations are on the wire—I can't have the Harringtons getting angry, or us looking like idiots.'

'I'm not sure,' Ben said as calmly as he could, 'what that has to do with me.'

'If you call Olivia a liar in the press, it will look bad on us and them.'

'How would it look bad on us?' Ben demanded. 'She's the one who lied.'

'You haven't seen the photos, I take it.'

'Photos?' Ben could feel his blood pressure skyrocket again. He took several more deep breaths. He was not going to get angry about stupid Olivia Harrington. He was not going to get angry about anything, not any more. He wouldn't let himself. 'What photos?' he asked evenly.

'Of you and Olivia getting busy in the hotel pool.'

'What...' He stopped abruptly, remembering how he'd held her by the shoulders. How her long, slender legs had tangled with his in the water. How he'd felt her breasts press against his arm when he'd towed her to the edge of the pool.

Damn it.

'I haven't seen the photos,' he said tersely, 'but trust me, nothing happened. She'd swallowed some pool water and I was helping to...'

'Resuscitate her?' Spencer finished, his voice edged with sarcasm, and Ben winced. All right, so it sounded lame. It was still the truth.

Sort of.

Because while nothing had happened between them last night, he'd still felt a powerful pulse of attraction towards her. He'd had trouble sleeping, all because he was picturing Olivia in that ridiculous skimpy swimsuit and how she'd look when he peeled it off her. It had been way too long since he'd been with a woman.

'So what do you want me to do?' he asked heavily, and Spencer didn't answer for a moment.

'For whatever reason, Olivia Harrington said you were dating,' he finally said. 'Maybe she has the hots for you.' And maybe not, although Ben didn't think he was imagining the sexual tension he'd felt between them last night. Not, of course, that either of them intended to do anything about it. He certainly didn't. He didn't trust himself with any kind of serious relationship, and a fling with a wild card like Olivia Harrington was just plain stupid.

'I want you to keep up the pretence of your relationship,' Spencer decided. 'Until the festival is over and this deal is closed.'

'You want me to pretend to be dating Olivia Harrington,' Ben clarified flatly. He could not believe his brother was actually asking him to do something so ludicrous.

'Yes,' Spencer said, as if it was both obvious and reasonable. 'That's the only solution, considering the circumstances.'

'No.'

'Ben. This deal is crucial to me. Uncle Gene already thinks it's in the bag...'

'And why does he think that?'

Spencer sighed. 'Because I thought it was. John Harrington, useless idiot that he is, told me it was. Help me out here, Ben. Please.'

'I'm already helping you out,' Ben pointed out. 'More than I even wanted to. This goes beyond, Spencer, what I am willing to do for the sake of The Chatsfield.'

'What about our family?' Spencer asked quietly. 'What would you do for them, Ben?'

'This isn't about family...'

'The hotel is always about the family, and the family is about the hotel,' Spencer said flatly. 'You know that, Ben, even if you don't like it. One fails or succeeds with the other.'

'I wouldn't,' Ben answered, 'call our family a success.'

'I know.' They were both silent for a minute, remembering the anger and pain of their childhood. All the arguing. All the insults and impatience from their father, all the mute misery from their mother. All the lies. 'This is all I've got,' Spencer said quietly, and Ben heard the ache of honesty in his voice. 'I've poured my life into this hotel, Ben. It *is* my family. I've made it so, for better or for worse.'

Ben didn't answer. He knew he'd done the same with his business. Used it to fill up the empty spaces, to channel all the emotion. He didn't have anything else in his life either.

'Please...'

'Okay.' He didn't need or want his brother to beg. 'Fine. I'll do it. But don't ask me for anything else, Spencer. I mean it.'

'I won't.'

Ben hung up the phone, stared into space for a while, memories of his childhood churning through him as he battled between anger and resignation. And tried not to think about pretending to be Olivia Harrington's boyfriend.

Olivia hurried through the lobby, keeping her sunglasses on celebrity-style and her head down low. Thank God she didn't see Ben anywhere, and she made it to the bank of elevators without running into anyone. She needed time to regroup and think of just how she was going to deal with Ben. What role she'd take with him.

The lift pinged open and she stepped inside, exhaling in relief to see it was empty. She'd just pushed the button for the floor of executive suites and the doors had started to close when a hand—a brown, masculine hand—slammed onto the door and forced it open. Olivia shrank back against the wall as Ben entered the lift.

'Well,' he drawled, his eyes two narrowed hazel

slits, his body radiating suppressed, lethal tension. 'Fancy meeting you here.'

Olivia managed a breezy smile even as her stomach clenched. And other parts of her clenched too, because even when he was angry—and Ben Chatsfield was definitely angry—he still looked almost unbearably sexy. The rumpled, just-got-out-of-bed hair. The designer stubble. The crooked tie. The dimple. All of it made Olivia take a deep breath and attempt to calm her raging hormones.

So he was sexy. Fine. She could deal with it. She'd have to deal with it, especially if she wanted to convince him to act like her boyfriend for the next ten days.

And just what would that entail?

'It's a small world, isn't it,' Olivia answered back, still trying for breezy. And succeeding, because she didn't think Ben could tell how nervous she was. His eyes remained narrowed and he folded his arms across that impressive chest and gave her a steady, smouldering stare. And not the good kind of smouldering.

'So,' he asked as the doors closed and they soared upwards, 'you weren't trying to avoid me, by any chance?'

Olivia widened her eyes in pseudo-innocence. 'Why on earth would I try to do that?'

'Because of the stunt you pulled this afternoon, perhaps?'

She hesitated, her mind racing as she considered how to play this. Light and flirty, or humble and contrite? What was likely to get Ben on her side?

The answer, Olivia suspected, was nothing.

'No answer for once?' Ben asked, one eyebrow cynically arched. 'Or are you just scrambling for a way to excuse your appalling behaviour?'

Ouch. Honesty it was then. 'I'm afraid I didn't think through what I was saying.'

His eyebrow arched higher and his mouth compressed. 'Oh, really? So you didn't tell the entire world's media that we were dating as some sort of revenge?'

He sounded so disbelieving that Olivia could only stare for a second. The doors pinged open and neither of them moved.

'This is my floor,' she said needlessly.

'I realise, since it used to be my floor.'

'Right.' She swallowed, and then smiled. She was going to go for light, at least for now. 'Would you like to come in, so we can discuss this reasonably?'

Ben's smile reminded her of a shark's. Not that she'd seen many sharks smile, or look so sexy.

'I'd love to,' he said.

Olivia's back prickled as Ben followed her to

her suite. She fumbled with her key card and skidded on the marble tile of the suite's foyer, nerves jangling inside her. She took a deep breath and turned around, gave him what she hoped was an appealing smile.

'Look, I realise this is awkward, and I also realise it's my fault.'

'I'm so relieved.' He stood in the doorway of the living room, one massive shoulder propped against the wall, his arms folded across his chest, making his biceps bulge and the expensive fabric of his suit stretch taut across his shoulders.

Even though he was completely still and self-contained, she felt the restlessness from him. The anger. Oh, dear. This was going to be rather difficult.

'I didn't tell the press we were dating as some sort of revenge,' she told him, keeping her voice light and playful with effort. 'What kind of revenge would that be anyway? You'd just deny it and I'd look like an idiot who had a crush on you.'

Ben inclined his head in acknowledgement. 'So why did you say it then?'

'Well, remember that look-before-you-leap thing?'

'You mean that you don't?'

She nodded sombrely even as her eyes sparkled at him, invited him to see the funny side of it. Because there was one, right? 'I'm afraid that's what happened this afternoon.'

Ben eyed her coolly. 'So you just happened to blurt out that we were dating? How did the subject even come up?'

'Have you seen the newspapers?'

His mouth hardened into a line and he shook his head. 'No, not yet.'

'Here.' She pulled a paper out of her shoulder bag and slapped it onto the table. 'Have a look.'

His jaw tight, Ben reached for the newspaper and snapped it open.

Olivia turned away, because she really didn't need to see those photos again. Isabelle had just called her, utterly furious about the story.

'How could you do this?' she'd demanded. 'He's a *Chatsfield*.'

'We're not seeing each other, Isabelle,' Olivia had explained wearily. 'It was just…an awkward moment.'

'And you should not be having any awkward moments with a Chatsfield!'

'What is this, *Romeo and Juliet*?' Olivia demanded sarcastically, although she'd been the one to invoke the Bard with that irritating reporter earlier. 'You're the one with the vendetta against the Chatsfields, Isabelle, not me.'

'So you don't care if they take over our family business?' Isabelle demanded, and Olivia had just kept herself from saying that maybe that would be a good thing. Maybe Isabelle would be happier if she didn't have the hotel to obsess over. Maybe Olivia would be happier if her family wasn't so concerned with the hotel, above everything else.

'I'm just saying we all need to calm down,' Olivia said instead, and Isabelle huffed.

'I'm very calm. But you need to fix this, Olivia. I don't need any bad press right now, okay?'

'Neither do I, as it happens,' Olivia answered. Her sister hadn't even asked how the festival was going. She, like everyone else in their family, didn't really care. At least it felt that way to Olivia. But maybe if she landed a real role, if she proved herself as an actress…

It would all be worth it. She'd show her family she was serious; she'd honour her mother's memory.

But you can't rewrite history, Olivia. You can't fix the mistakes you've already made.

No, but she could orient everything in her life so she wouldn't make the same mistakes again.

'How did this happen?' Ben bit out, tossing the paper back onto the table like so much trash. He paced the room like a caged tiger, one hand driven through his hair. 'We were in a private space, a rooftop pool…'

'Telephoto lens from another building,' Olivia answered with a shrug. 'That's my best guess.'

He whirled on her, his face suffused with barely leashed anger. 'And a reporter just happened to be there, at nearly midnight?'

She drew back at the implication. 'Are you accusing me of setting you up? Why would I?'

'Why would I give you a supply closet for a room?' Ben practically snarled.

Olivia took a deep breath and let it out slowly. 'I already apologised for the assumption I made about the room.'

He stood there rigidly for a moment, and then the anger left his face and body as if he were willing it away. He raked a hand through his hair, letting out a long, low breath. 'And I apologised for the things I said to you last night.'

'You mean, self-important, shallow wannabe actress?' she couldn't help but remind him.

'That would be them,' he agreed without so much as a wince.

'Okay, so apologies have been made and accepted. And I think we can agree that neither of us is out to get the other. Right?'

He eyed her warily for a long moment and Olivia just kept herself from rolling her eyes in response. Seriously?

'Right,' he finally said, and she nodded and pointed to the paper, deciding brisk and business-like was best.

'Now about this—I need to ask a favour.'

Ben's gaze narrowed. 'Oh?'

'It would be awkward for me to admit I made a mistake in saying we were dating.'

'To admit you were telling a bald-faced lie, you mean,' Ben returned, a sharp edge to his voice, and Olivia suppressed the flare of irritation she felt and gave him a wry smile instead. She'd charm him into agreeing. As dubious a prospect as that seemed, it was also the only one she could think of right now.

'Well, if you want to put it that way, yes.'

'So let me guess.' Ben folded his arms. 'You want me to agree to this sham of a relationship until—when? The festival is over?'

'That would be fantastic,' Olivia agreed cautiously. Ben had cottoned on just a little too quickly to her plan for her to feel comfortable. She was waiting for the catch. 'I have a film deal in the works,' she explained after a pause, 'and it's important that nothing messes it up.'

'And how would your personal life affect a film deal?'

She shrugged. 'Hollywood politics. This is a serious film, award-winning stuff. They don't want an actress involved who whips up a media frenzy with tabloid photos and then…'

'Lies about them.'

She gritted her teeth. 'Right.'

Ben cocked his head, swept her with a coolly

assessing gaze. 'So what would play-acting at dating involve?'

'Nothing much,' Olivia said quickly. She willed herself not to blush and to stop thinking about what it most definitely wouldn't involve. Like kissing him. 'A couple of appearances, tops.'

'A couple.'

'I have a film premiere tomorrow night. Naturally people would expect us to go together. And maybe we could be seen out once—having dinner or a party or something?'

'And that's it?'

'Since you obviously can't bear the thought of spending any more time with me than necessary,' she retorted, 'yes, that's it.' She'd meant to sound wry and light and instead had come across as a bitter old hag. Oops.

'Well…' Ben gave one short, terse nod. 'I suppose I can manage that.'

'Really?' Not in her wildest dreams had she expected him to be so accommodating. What she'd really been expecting was for him to tell her to deal with it on her own, because he wouldn't be helping her get out of the huge hole she'd dug all by herself. So naturally she felt just a little suspicious. 'You're sure you're okay with this?' she probed carefully.

Ben's jaw locked. 'I said I was, but it's hardly ideal. I hate any kind of play-acting. Lying to anyone, much less the entire world, is not something I relish.' His mouth had hardened into a thin line and he looked angry again. Olivia swallowed.

'Well, thank you. I appreciate your understanding in this, uh, matter.'

'It shouldn't be too arduous,' he answered, and stupidly, Olivia felt herself blush. She was imagining what their sham relationship could involve that would be *arduous*. Energetic. Passionate.

She glanced at Ben, and with a thrill of shock she saw a heat simmering in his eyes, felt the air tauten and snap with tension between them. *Sexual* tension. This little charade might prove to be more of a challenge than she'd anticipated.

More of a temptation.

'So…the premiere tomorrow night. You're up for that?'

'I suppose I'll have to be. What does it entail exactly?'

'We'll appear on the red carpet together for a photo op…' Ben grimaced and she frowned. 'There's no point if we don't have photos taken,' she said, and he shrugged.

'Fine.'

She felt his derision like a physical thing, as if he'd slung a bucket of mud over her. She felt dirty.

'We need to show the public…'

'That we're dating. Yes, I realise. As I said before, I just don't like play-acting.'

Which must make her career choice particularly repugnant, Olivia thought. This was a match made in heaven. Not.

'So a couple of photos, we watch the movie, and then there's an after party. We can keep it short though.' Even though she should be there, rubbing shoulders and mingling. Networking.

'Fine.'

She swallowed, nodded. Tried to imagine what a date, even a pretend one, would feel like with Ben. Her mind leaped ahead to other scenarios, impossible ones of Ben kissing her. Backing her up against a door and pressing that long, lean, hard body against hers. That mobile mouth, now compressed into a hard line, against hers. Heat flared in her face and pooled in her belly. She glanced at Ben and saw him staring at her with so much answering heat that she nearly took a step backwards. Reminded herself that Ben Chatsfield was a dangerous proposition for someone who didn't do relationships or even flings. Someone who needed to focus on her career.

Her brain kept saying that, but her body didn't seem to be listening.

'See you tomorrow,' she managed, her voice little more than a squeak, and with one abrupt nod Ben turned on his heel and left her suite.

CHAPTER FOUR

OLIVIA STARED AT her reflection with narrowed eyes. Her make-up was understated, just a little eyeliner and natural lipstick. She'd splurged on a blowout that afternoon, and her hair fell in perfect glossy waves, or at least would until the icy rain needling Berlin in February would turn it into a bedraggled, matted mess. As for her dress…

She turned this way and that, checking to see how far her hemline jerked up when she moved. It was a fine line between sexy and confident and professional and mature, without roving into demure or dull territory. She hoped this silver slip dress with the skinny straps and swingy skirt hit the right note. It had certainly cost enough.

She slipped her feet into a pair of silver stilettos and did a little twirl. Darn, had she just flashed her underwear? She wouldn't be doing that again.

Her nerves jangled as she took her little black

diamante-spangled clutch and made sure it held all the basics: lipstick, tissues, key card, debit card, phone. She was good. A deep breath and then another, and she resisted the temptation of indulging in a little Dutch courage—the executive suite had a fully stocked minibar—because alcohol had always gone to her head and if ever she needed all her wits about her...

Tonight was important, the premiere of the first serious film she'd had a supporting role in. Okay, twenty lines was not a lot. But she was on screen for a lot longer; she was going to be seen, and with the negotiations still going on for the role she really wanted, the role that would make her career, that would finally prove to her family and to herself that she'd made the right choice, that it had all been worth it, that *she* was worth something...she knew she couldn't afford to mess this up.

Which meant making sure the whole world believed she and Ben Chatsfield were really dating.

And with that thought still sending alarm bells pealing through her brain, the doorbell to her suite rang.

She put on her airiest, most insouciant smile as she opened the door, and the breath bottled in her lungs came out in a rush as she caught sight of Ben. He wore a grey silk suit, the streamlined jacket and narrow trousers emphasising his incredible physique. He'd opted to go without a tie, and the top button of his crisp white shirt was undone. Olivia could not quite tear her gaze away from the lean, perfect column of his throat. The nerves that had been jangling through her all seemed to coalesce into a hot ball of longing in her stomach. She pressed one hand against her middle and then dropped it, afraid she'd revealed too much already by the way she was staring at him as if he were a chocolate-fudge sundae and someone had just handed her a spoon.

'You look…' She licked her lips and then forced her smile back into place. 'Great. We match.'

His gaze roved over her, taking in the silver dress that now definitely felt too short. Too sexy.

'So do you. Look great, that is.' He spoke abruptly, as if he wasn't used to giving compliments but had been compelled to honesty, which for some reason made Olivia smile.

'Thanks.' She grabbed her clutch and started out; Ben stayed her with one hand.

'Don't you want a coat? It's freezing outside.'

'A parka would kind of ruin my red-carpet moment.'

'You could always leave it in the car.'

'I thought we'd just take a cab…' She couldn't afford anything else. This festival was already straining her modest budget.

'Good thing I hired a limo, then.'

Shock had her going rigid, her jaw dropping before she thought to snap it shut. 'You did?'

He shrugged. 'If we're going to do it, let's do it right.'

'That—that was very thoughtful of you,' she said. She was absurdly touched that Ben had considered doing anything above showing up. She knew he didn't want to be here, didn't want to pretend, but he had still gone the extra distance.

He shrugged again, as if he weren't used to compliments. 'It wasn't a big deal.'

Olivia grabbed her coat, glad for its warmth as they left the hotel and stepped out into a sleeting February night. 'I don't understand why Berlin holds their film festival in February,' she told him as she tried not to let her teeth chatter. 'I'd much prefer July.'

'I have to agree with you there.' Ben reached across her to open the door of the sleek black limo idling in front of the hotel, and Olivia felt a thrill run through her, both from the fact that she would be arriving at the premiere in a limo, and the closeness of Ben's body next to hers. She could smell his aftershave, something clean and woodsy, feel the heat emanating from him, and that alone was enough to send little jolts of awareness through her system.

'Where do you live normally?' she asked as she slid into the sumptuous leather interior of the limo. Ben slid in next to her, his thigh nudging hers before he sat back and left a good foot between them. Stupid to feel disappointed about *that*.

'Nice.'

'As in France?'

'That's the one.'

'You know, until that stupid thing in the newspaper, I didn't realise you were a celebrity chef.'

He made a face. 'I hate that term.'

'But you are,' Olivia persisted with a teasing smile. 'Ben's Bistro is big stuff. I tried to get into the one in London once and the waiting list was a mile long.'

'Sorry.'

'You should be glad of your success,' she told him. Ambition was something she understood.

'I am.'

'So, a chef.' She shook her head slowly as he arched an eyebrow, his mouth curving into a slow, surprising and oh-so-sexy smile. She realised he didn't smile a lot. She liked it when he did.

'You're surprised?' he asked.

'I have to admit I had you pegged as a corporate type.' Although she supposed she shouldn't have, not with that wildness running through him. That leashed energy still fascinated her, still made her see Ben as dangerous and thrilling and far too much of a temptation.

'No way.' He stretched his legs out as he shook his head. 'Two weeks managing a hotel is bad enough.'

'Why did you agree, then?'

The smile left his face and he turned to look out the window. 'It was a favour to my brother.'

'Which one?'

'Spencer.'

'And why can't he be here?'

'I think he had a little business to attend to in New York.'

'You mean The Harrington.' She should have realised that a long time ago.

He turned to look at her, his mouth quirking in something not quite a smile. 'You're not involved in the family business?'

'You're not either,' she shot back before she could think better of it. Ben just raised his eyebrows and she realised how prickly and defensive she'd sounded. 'No, I never have been,' she admitted, her tone thankfully more even. 'It was always Isabelle and John's thing. Eleanore's too, I suppose.'

'Your siblings.'

'Yes. John and Isabelle do the managing and Eleanore's into design.'

'And you?' Ben asked quietly, with just a little too much perception.

'I act.' And had been acting since she was

twelve years old, when she realised she didn't like who she really was. Escaping into someone else was so much easier, and it was something that, strangely perhaps, made her feel closer to her mother. Closer, sadly, than when she'd just been herself.

'What about you?' she asked. 'How come you haven't been involved in The Chatsfield?'

His mouth tightened and one hand clenched into a fist on his thigh. 'It was never my thing.'

'But you started your own restaurants? Surely that could go hand in hand with the hotelier business?'

'Could,' he agreed evenly. He looked out through the sleet that was now coming down horizontally. 'It's nasty out. But we're almost there.'

'Okay.' Nerves fluttered in her stomach. How this film was received, how she was received, could make or break her.

Ben shot her a surprisingly sympathetic look. 'You don't need to be nervous. You really do look great.'

Olivia pressed a hand to her chest. 'Thank you,' she said quietly. 'It's just that so much rides on this evening.'

'This other film you're hoping to be in, right?'

'Yes. I've been waiting years for an opportunity like this one, and I really don't want to blow it.' She heard the anxiety as well as the eagerness in her voice and inwardly winced. She sounded so pathetic.

Ben met her gaze steadily. 'You won't.'

He sounded so certain that Olivia actually felt her nervousness ease slightly. She smiled at him, grateful for his faith in her, unlikely as it was.

'Thank you,' she said again, meaning it more than she could articulate, and then the limo pulled over to the kerb and one of the theatre's staff opened the door, holding an umbrella aloft. With a last, fleeting smile for Ben, Olivia shrugged out of her parka and slipped out of the car.

Ben slid out of the limo, watching as Olivia waved to the fans lining the roped-off red carpet. Flash-bulbs popped and paparazzi started calling out—or rather, shrieking—questions.

'When did you start dating Ben Chatsfield?'

'How did you two meet?'

'How do you feel about The Chatsfield's bid to take over The Harrington?'

Ben felt Olivia stiffen next to him, even though her smile didn't slip. The woman was a professional. It had to be seriously annoying though, he thought, to be barraged by questions about her fake romance instead of her career—a career she clearly cared about and was working hard for. Back in the limo he'd felt a glimmer of understanding and even compassion for her, and he felt it even more now.

God knew he understood how much you could want something. And like him Olivia had ambition and dreams, and a desire to prove herself— just as he had.

And that twinge of sympathy made him slip his hand into hers and smile for the blasted cameras. 'Olivia doesn't want to talk about us tonight,' he told the reporters, keeping his voice jokey and light so they wouldn't feel the dismissal. 'She wants to talk about the film…' For a moment his brain went blank but then thankfully memory kicked in and he continued smoothly, '*Blue Skies Forever*. I can't wait to see it myself.'

The reporters started with their questions again and sliding his arm around her waist, his fingers splayed against her hip, Ben began to walk towards the theatre.

'Thank you,' Olivia murmured when they'd passed the last reporter and made it to the lobby of the theatre.

'All part of the service.'

She turned to him, smiling, but with her eyes narrowed. 'Why are you being so nice again? Because I don't think I've actually endeared myself to you.'

He let out a laugh, enjoying her candour. And the view. That little silver dress she wore? It was *little*. And it showcased her long, tanned, slim legs in a way that made Ben want to run his hand down them and back up again.

'I'm a nice guy?'

'Not sure I'm buying that one.'

He decided to come clean, not that he'd actually been hiding all that much. 'As it happens, my brother would like this charade to continue as well.'

She frowned. 'You mean Spencer? Why does he care?'

'Because any bad publicity, especially with a Harrington, wouldn't be good right about now.'

'You mean because he's still trying to buy The Harrington.'

She sighed, more in weariness than anger, and Ben asked curiously, 'Do you care about it? I mean, do you want to keep it in the family?' They'd both steered clear of family politics earlier, but they'd also both admitted to not having any interest in their respective family hotels.

Which wasn't exactly true on his part. He didn't know what he felt for The Chatsfield, family or hotel, but he knew his feelings were too complicated to be dismissed.

'I don't know.' Olivia shrugged, her forehead puckering. 'I've never been that interested in it, but it's always been there.' She hesitated, a shadow crossing her features as she shot him an uncertain look. 'Sometimes I think we'd all be better off without it. The pressure Isabelle is under…and John…' She bit her lip and shook her head. 'But I shouldn't be talking to you about this. Technically, you're the enemy.'

'Technically, I'm also supposed to be your boyfriend.'

'Yeah, it's kind of complicated, isn't it?' She let out a little laugh and shook her head. 'What on earth was I thinking, blurting out that we were dating?'

'I think you weren't thinking, remember?'

'Right.' She shook her head again, and then gave him a playful smile that made his insides sizzle. His libido was clearly in hyperdrive after being on ice for a while. He'd been so focused on building his business and keeping his emotions under control…he'd indulged in the occasional fling or one-night stand, but not recently, and his body was reminding him of that now. Painfully.

'So your willingness to agree yesterday,' she said, wagging a finger at him, 'was really just because your brother made you do it.'

Ben felt himself tense, the familiar anger rushing through him. Fingers into fists. Shoulders hunched. He took a deep breath, forced himself to relax. 'My brother doesn't make me do anything,' he said, and his voice came out easy and light. 'Like I said, it's a favour.'

'Ladies and gentlemen, please take your seats in the theatre.'

Now Olivia was the one who was tensing, and without even thinking too much about what he was doing Ben took her hand. 'Come on,' he said as he tugged her along. 'You want to be in the front row, don't you?'

'I don't know,' she muttered, her gaze darting to the people around her. An actress Ben vaguely recognised came up to her and kissed her on both cheeks.

'Olivia! So nice to see you. Can't wait to see the finished product, can you?'

To her credit Olivia straightened, her anxiety vanishing completely as she gave the woman a dazzling smile. 'No, I can't. It's been a long time coming, hasn't it?'

'Who was that?' Ben asked as Olivia waggled her fingers at the actress and they moved towards the theatre.

'Liz Chellis?' She gave him a look of smiling disbelief. 'Only one of the most famous actresses in the world right now.'

'I thought I recognised her.'

She laughed and shook her head, and then they took their seats of red plush velvet—in the third row.

'Don't want to look too eager,' Olivia whispered, and Ben nodded.

'Wise move,' he whispered back, and then they didn't have time to talk any more because the lights were dimming and the film started.

Ben hadn't really thought much, or at all, about the film he'd be seeing. He'd been focused on navigating what was going to be a tricky piece of theatre—and he was no actor. He'd also been trying not to get too bothered about the fakery of the whole thing, because while he hated the idea of it, he recognised the need. But it still felt like lying.

It *was* lying.

So all that had taken up his headspace and he hadn't thought about Olivia's movie at all.

Yet within the first few minutes of the film starting, he found himself caught up in the story. It was a Depression-era period drama, moody and full of sweeping shots of the American plains, and Olivia, he decided, looked pretty fine in checked gingham, her hair blowing in the relentless, dust-ridden wind.

Yet looks aside, she captivated him. Her character was the oldest daughter of the main character, a woman struggling to make ends meet after her husband struck out for Chicago to find work, and while Olivia didn't have that many lines, when she came onto the screen she took it over with her quiet dignity, her heartfelt delivery. He *believed* she was Grace Wilton, an eighteen-year-old girl who had run out of hope. He even wanted to make her believe again.

The depth of his own emotion surprised him. Embarrassed him, even. When had he last felt so much about a stupid movie? Yet he couldn't take his eyes off Olivia on the screen…or the woman sitting next to him.

He glanced at her every few minutes throughout the film, and although she was smiling and looking relaxed, he could see how tightly she clenched the armrests. She was a good actress, he thought with amusement, but not that good.

And when the lights went up she let out a gusty sigh of relief.

'Was that enjoyable,' he asked in a low voice, 'or torture?'

'A bit of both.' She turned to him, as breezy as ever, yet Ben saw a touching vulnerability in her chocolate-brown eyes. 'Well? Dare I ask what you thought?'

'I thought it was great. Actually,' Ben corrected, 'I thought *you* were great. The movie got a little moody and self-consciously deep towards the middle, but I really believed you were Grace Wilton.'

'You did?'

'Don't sound so surprised.'

'No, it's just…' She fiddled with the simple silver pendant she wore around her neck, a heart whose edges overlapped. 'I don't know what to do when you act nicely.'

'Act nicely back?' Ben suggested, and was intrigued to see colour touch Olivia's cheekbones. Were they flirting? Just how nice did he want Olivia to be?

Very, very nice.

'Come on,' he said, pushing that thought away. The last thing he needed was to complicate something that was already pretty damn complicated. 'I think everyone's going back out to the lobby.'

'There's a bit of an after party,' Olivia said as they headed out of the theatre. 'Do you mind?'

'It's fine.'

But it wasn't as fine as he'd hoped it would be. An hour of small talk and schmoozing was an hour more than he liked. He hated this kind of fake socialising, made all the more fake by his supposed relationship with Olivia. Posing for a single photo felt different than chatting to a bunch of people Ben didn't know and making stuff up about him and Olivia.

Well, he wasn't making stuff up. She was. And she did a damn good job of it, which, unreasonably, he knew, annoyed him.

He'd had too much bad experience with lies. With believing them. And he didn't want Olivia to be a good liar, even though he could already see that she was.

'It was a bit of opposites attract, really,' she said, her arm linked through Ben's as she chatted with several Hollywood types Ben thought he recognised but couldn't name, even though he'd been introduced to them fifteen minutes ago. 'Wasn't it, sweetheart?'

'Definitely.' He gave the little crowd an eye roll and a smile, squeezing Olivia's arm and pulling her closer even though everything in him rebelled against this play-acting. 'Let's just say sparks flew.'

'And the whole hotel thing?' a woman asked, eyebrows raised. Ben tensed, and felt Olivia do the same. Neither of them, he suspected, really wanted to talk about the whole hotel thing. 'I suppose you have that in common.'

'Oh.' Olivia relaxed. 'Yes, our childhoods were amazingly similar, weren't they, Ben? Birthday dinners in the hotel dining room…hide-and-seek in the hallways…' She gave him a soppy smile and he managed some sort of smile back.

'Yeah. Right.'

Thankfully the conversation moved on to Hollywood, which was a relief, and Ben let the words drift over him as he considered what Olivia had said. Did they have similar childhoods? He'd had a few birthday dinners in The Chatsfield, London. It had meant to be a treat, but it had stopped feeling like one after a while.

He didn't care about that though. What he'd cared about—what he was bitter about, *still*—was how the birthday dinners and the hide-and-seek in the hallways and the appearance in front of the hotel's entrance, waving at the crowds, had all been an illusion. A trick to make everyone believe the Chatsfields were one big happy family. He'd known the truth, had heard it in the arguments his parents had had at home, in the way his father's mouth had twisted every time he'd looked at Spencer.

And yet still Ben had bought into the illusion, had tried to make it real by pleasing everyone, smoothing over every argument, trying so damn hard. And then his father had told him the truth and he'd realised there had been no point. There had never been any point. And maybe everyone, himself included, would have been better off if he hadn't been such a damn Boy Scout and tried to make everyone happy.

Ben felt the tension knot in his shoulders as the memories came rushing back, spurred by just a few simple words of Olivia's. He was tired and hungry—he'd skipped dinner to attend this thing—and he was also fed up with pretending. He was fed up with all the thoughts that raced through his head, emotions that churned in his gut. Coming back to The Chatsfield was hard—

and pretending to be Olivia Harrington's boyfriend wasn't making his life any easier.

When there was a break in the conversation he bent his head to murmur in Olivia's ear, 'Shall we go?'

She glanced up at him, her face flushed, her eyes sparkling. She was enjoying this, he realised. This was her crowd, her moment, and while he felt a flicker of remorse for taking her away from it, he still knew he needed to leave.

'Sure. Of course,' she said, and then spent another fifteen minutes saying her effusive goodbyes to everyone. Ben waited, his hands jammed in his pockets, the tension inside him coiling tighter and tighter, ready to snap. He felt as if everything were pressing in on him—the charade with Olivia, the memories of The Chatsfield, Spencer's expectations. He needed to swim about a million laps.

'I'm ready,' Olivia said with a brilliant smile that was definitely not for his benefit, and they headed out into the rainy night.

The paparazzi were still waiting like vultures outside the theatre.

'Olivia! Ben! How was your date?'

Ben fully intended to shoulder past them, but Olivia hesitated. She probably wanted someone to ask about the film, but of course they weren't going to. They wanted a money shot, that was all.

'How about a kiss?' someone called, and after a tiny pause she turned to Ben, a playful smile curving her lips.

No. No, no, no. He was not going to kiss her in front of all these bozos. He was not going to kiss her just because some annoying reporter asked him to. He wouldn't be that fake.

No, Ben realised, but she was going to kiss him. With that playful smile still flirting with her mouth she stepped forward and slid her arms around his neck. He felt her breasts press against his chest, and the slippery, silvery fabric of her dress suddenly seemed like very little barrier between them. Out of instinct he steadied her by putting his hands on her hips, and then she reached up on her tiptoes and kissed him.

Her lips brushed against his in a feather-soft kiss, not much of a kiss at all, really, and yet it ignited a firestorm inside Ben so that he tightened his hands on her hips and pulled her against his very noticeable arousal.

Every thought and resolution he'd had flew out of his head as he plundered her mouth, his tongue slipping inside her softness, and he felt the little pulse of shock that went through her.

Felt it in himself. *What the hell was he doing?*

Far too abruptly, Ben thrust her away from him. Olivia looked shocked, her mouth a little swollen, her hair damp and curling in the rain. A reporter wolf whistled, and furious with both her and himself, Ben stalked to the limo without waiting to see if she followed.

CHAPTER FIVE

THE MAN COULD KISS. That wildness that Olivia had suspected hid under his controlled exterior? She'd just had a taste of it, and it had left her mind whirling and her lips—and other parts of her body—throbbing.

Bemused, Olivia followed Ben towards the limo. She barely heard the shouts of the reporters, or saw the flashbulbs going off.

She'd never been kissed like that before. She'd hardly been kissed at all.

Not, of course, that she was going to tell Ben that.

But it had been some kiss. And one she'd wanted, had been thinking about all night. Even longer, if she were honest with herself. And when the reporters had asked for a kiss…well, Olivia hadn't been about to say no. She'd wanted to kiss him too much, and the request was no more than an excuse to touch him. Taste him.

And he'd tasted good.

She slid into the limo, saw that Ben was sitting

on the far side, his face turned determinedly towards the window.

Olivia thought about making some wry comment about the kiss, joking about it even, but she couldn't quite make herself do it. The kiss had been wonderful, but the way he'd thrust her away from him afterwards...

Well, that had been a little ego-bruising. She wasn't sure why he'd done it, and she'd didn't think she could pull off the breezy confidence to ask. Not when she had so little experience with kisses, and especially kisses like that.

They didn't talk for the ten minutes it took to get back to The Chatsfield, which just made everything more awkward. But the moment had passed for Olivia to make some light joke, and now if she mentioned the kiss it would sound cringingly rehearsed and serious, as if she cared too much. Maybe she should just let it go, and the next time they saw each other things would be normal.

Whatever that looked like.

A bellhop opened the door as the limo pulled up outside The Chatsfield. Ben slid out first, but at least had the grace to wait for Olivia to exit the car.

'So,' she said as they came into the art-nouveau lobby with its lashings of marble and gilt. People bustled around them and she could hear the tinkling of piano music from the bar, the muted ping of the elevator doors opening and closing.

'So.' Ben thrust his hands in his pockets, his gaze not meeting hers. 'Let me know when you next need me. A party, you said, right?'

'Or we could go out to dinner.' Although the idea of spending several hours alone with him made her feel queasy with both nerves and anticipation. It could be all kinds of awkward...and yet she knew she wanted to see him again. *Kiss him again.*

'Whatever. Just leave a message with my PA if you can't reach me.' And without a backwards glance, he strode away from her towards his office.

Okay. Olivia stood there for a moment, knowing it was silly to feel dismissed or even rejected, and yet feeling it all the same.

This isn't real, Olivia? Remember?

Of course she remembered. She'd dated two aspiring actors before, as her agent Melissa had suggested she do, and those relationships had been as fake as this one. They'd met up for dinner or drinks to keep reporters interested and their names known. They hadn't loved or even liked each other. It had been, Olivia acknowledged, a simple matter of expediency.

Just like this thing with Ben was.

Except, she realised as she headed up to her

suite, she'd actually enjoyed herself with Ben tonight. He'd made her laugh and he'd helped her to relax. He'd listened to her and when he'd kissed her…

Okay, maybe she should stop thinking about that. Because obviously this thing with Ben was going nowhere. He was a Chatsfield, she was a Harrington. She was pretty sure, tonight aside, he didn't really like her. And she wasn't looking to get involved with anyone anyway. She had her career to think about and she'd already resolved not to have any serious relationships. She simply didn't trust herself enough for one.

As for casual…as tempting as a fling might be, she had a feeling Ben Chatsfield would chew her up, and then spit her out. She wasn't experienced enough to handle a fling with a man like him.

But she might convince herself she was if it meant he'd kiss her again.

With a weary sigh Olivia stripped off her silver dress and ran a huge bubble bath. She'd need all her energy for the run of festival events tomorrow. A charity lunch, an afternoon premiere of a documentary, a cocktail party in the evening. She needed to be on, on, on, which was how she liked it.

Except tonight, with Ben, she'd actually been herself. Mostly.

Another reason this thing between them wasn't going anywhere. She didn't *do* real.

Closing her eyes, Olivia sank into the froth of bubbles, determined not to think about Ben—or the way he'd kissed—again that night.

Several hours later she was lying in the huge king-size bed staring at the ceiling as she relived those precious seconds when Ben had taken control of their kiss. The way his hands had felt on her hips…his tongue sliding into her mouth…

She let out a shudder. All that raw passion directed at her…that had been as exciting as the actual feel of his tongue and lips.

Why, Olivia wondered, had it been so exciting? Maybe because so much of her life was a performance; Ben's response had been real. And maybe she craved just a little bit—or even a whole lot—of real.

But why had he thrust her away from him like that? Was he angry that he'd enjoyed the kiss? He had enjoyed it, of that she was sure. She'd felt the evidence, and that had thrilled her too.

But then he'd acted so disgusted, so *angry*… She wondered with an icy pang of anxiety if the gossip rags would decide to go with the 'trouble in paradise' theme rather than the hearts and roses Olivia had been hoping for?

Knowing she wouldn't sleep now, Olivia got up from the bed and went into the living room where she'd left her laptop. She powered it up and clicked on a few of the celebrity gossip sites before she found what she was looking for.

Or rather, what she *wasn't* looking for.

A photo of Ben pushing her away from him, his features tight with—what? Anger? Disgust? Whatever it was, it didn't look good, and the gossip site had run with it. *Relationship Already on the Rocks?* the headline blazed. Olivia scanned the article, saw there was nothing, absolutely nothing, about her film or her career. In fact, the whole article was aimed more for fans of Ben Chatsfield, the 'sexy restaurateur' who was 'apparently seeing aspiring actress Olivia Harrington.' Aspiring. She was not *aspiring*. She'd been in half a dozen films and she had a major role coming up.

Grimacing in disgust, Olivia shut her laptop and swung around to stare out the wraparound windows at the night sky. It was still raining, and the drops trickled down the angled windowpanes like tears.

She couldn't stay here and fume. She needed to know just why Ben had pushed her away—and what they were going to do about it now. Damage control. And since she'd been impulsive with Ben before, she might as well run with it.

Abruptly Olivia stood up and grabbed a dressing gown. She knotted it tightly around her waist before she marched out of her suite.

Two minutes later she stood in front of the door of her former bedroom, where Ben had intimated he was staying. She hoped he really was staying there, because it was two o'clock in the morning and she didn't fancy waking some stranger up.

She knocked. Loudly.

After a tense minute or so she heard low, annoyed mumbling, and then the sound of a knee or elbow connecting with something hard, followed by a savage curse. Then the door swung open, and Ben stood there, squinting in the light from the hall, his hair sticking up in every direction, wearing nothing but boxer shorts.

The breath dried in Olivia's lungs. Every rational thought—and there hadn't been many to begin with at this point in time—flew from her head. She stared at Ben with his bedhead and stubble and six-pack abs and felt a wave of longing crash over her with the force of a tsunami. And she knew she'd been fooling herself, thinking she wanted to wake him up in the middle of the night so they could discuss damage control. She'd come here because she wanted to be kissed.

Ben rubbed a hand over his face, blinking as if he couldn't believe she was really there. *'Olivia?'*

'Yes…' She took a step forward, jutting her chin, and decided to go on the attack. Surely that would be better than throwing herself at him. 'Why did you push me away tonight?'

He blinked some more. 'Push you away?'

'After—after you kissed me.'

He arched an eyebrow, turning supremely disdainful and even arrogant, despite the bedhead and boxers. 'As I recall, *you* kissed *me*.'

'So what if I did? You obviously enjoyed it.' The words were out of her mouth before she could think better of them, and Olivia saw Ben's eyes flare with awareness, felt the answering heat in herself. Uh-oh. 'And then you pushed me away like you couldn't stand the sight of me,' she continued, aware that she was babbling in her nervousness. 'And guess what the paparazzi decided to go for?'

'You mean they've already published some photos?'

'I checked one of the celebrity gossip sites tonight.'

He shook his head slowly, looking both incredulous and disgusted—although at the gossip sites or her for checking them, Olivia didn't know.

'So why did you?' she demanded.

'Why do you care?'

'Because of the photos. They're already wondering if we're legit...'

He folded his arms across his chest, muscles rippling impressively. He looked very bare and sleek and warm, and Olivia ached to touch him. Her hand flexed instinctively and she tried to take a step backwards, but some corner of her brain— or perhaps a different part of her body—must have been in revolt because she took a step forward instead, straight into Ben's chest.

His hands came up to grip her shoulders, and for a heart-stopping second she thought he'd push her away from him. Again.

And maybe he thought it too, for he held her still there for a moment, a moment that seemed to stretch on and on and yet last no time at all, for suddenly, so suddenly, he hauled her against him and he was kissing her the way he had earlier that night.

No, better, because there was no one watching, no need to restrain that wildness she'd known was in him, the crazy, uncontrollable and very real need whose answer she felt in herself.

His mouth devoured hers, his hands roving over her body, tugging at her robe, before she had a chance to so much as take a breath.

His hands came down to cup her bottom as he took a step backwards into the room and shut the door with one foot. Olivia was barely aware of his movements; her mind was a rushing torrent of sensations, from his tongue exploring her mouth to the hand that slid from her bottom to the sash of her dressing gown, undoing it with one swift tug before he slipped his hand under her cami top and cupped her bare breast. Olivia swayed where she stood.

And then, just like in her fantasy, Ben was backing her hard against the door, her spine hitting the handle with a painful bump that she barely registered. He pulled at her clothes, his movements abrupt, his breathing ragged, and desire raged through Olivia hard and hot and fast. Her breath hitched as Ben slid one hand into her pyjama pants and then yanked them down.

Good Lord. She bucked under his hand, her breath coming out in a rush as she sagged against the door, helpless under the onslaught of his knowing fingers.

He slid a finger inside her and Olivia let out a little moan. She could feel the hard press of his arousal against her, and she knew if she didn't stop this now she wouldn't possess the will power to. And she needed to, because she knew where this was going, fast, and she wasn't ready to go there yet.

Weakly but resolutely, she pushed against his chest. 'Ben.'

He stopped instantly, as if she'd flicked a switch, withdrawing his hand and stepping back. His face was flushed, his eyes dazed, and he shook his head as if to clear it. 'Sorry.' He looked down at her as if wondering how she'd got there. 'Sorry,' he said again.

Olivia adjusted her pyjamas and tied her robe. Her body buzzed with the aftershocks of his touch, and ached with unfulfilled longing. She cleared her throat.

'It's not that I don't want…' she began, and bit her lip. How much to say? To admit?

'You don't need to explain,' Ben said tersely. 'I was…out of control.'

His admission just added to the ache of unfulfilled longing. 'I kind of liked that,' she confessed shakily. 'But I'm not sure…'

'I know.' To her surprise he offered a wry smile. 'But I guess now we're even. You kissed me and now I kissed you.'

She smiled back. 'That was a little more than a kiss.'

His knowing gaze dropped to her chest, where her nipples were still peaked and pressed against her thin cami. 'Just a bit.'

Blushing, Olivia fiddled with the sash of her robe. 'Okay. Well.'

Ben raked a hand through his hair, making it stand up even more. 'Are you hungry?' he asked.

Olivia blinked at him. 'What?'

'I skipped dinner. I thought there would be more than rabbit food at that party.'

'There's never food at celebrity events. No one eats.'

'Well, I do. And I'm hungry.'

'Okay…'

'If you let me use the kitchen of your suite, I can make us a couple of omelettes.'

'My kitchen? I don't think I have any food…'

'Have you looked in the fridge?'

'No.'

'There's food. I left it in there.' Which reminded her that it had really been his suite, and he was now sleeping in this tiny closet of a bedroom, and really, Ben Chatsfield, despite the glower and the temper and the occasional insult, was a nice guy. Plus he was offering to make her food after he'd kissed her senseless and she'd pushed him away.

She could like this man.

Don't go there, Olivia. Don't even think about it.

'Okay. An omelette sounds great.' Because she actually was starving, now that she thought about it, and…well, she didn't want to go back and stare at the ceiling all night by herself, wondering just what was going on between her and Ben Chatsfield, if anything.

Back in her suite—or really, Ben's suite—he made himself at home in the kitchen. He'd put on a pair of faded jeans over his boxers and a worn grey T-shirt to cover up that amazing chest, and he looked, Olivia decided after some leisurely perusal, just as sexy in those beat-up clothes as he had in a tailored suit. Maybe more.

She slid onto a high bar stool and watched as he cracked six eggs into a bowl one-handed and then whisked them to a froth.

'So how did you come to be a chef?' she asked. He'd retrieved a bell pepper and some mushrooms from the fridge—which now that she'd had a peek inside she could see was well stocked—and started dicing them with lightning-quick precision.

'I fell into it.'

'You mean you weren't whipping up cupcakes as a boy?' she teased, and he gave her a narrowed look.

'I'm a chef, not a baker.'

'Same difference, right?'

'No.' He took an omelette pan from under the stove and tossed a knob of butter into it.

'All right, so how did you fall into it?'

He hesitated, and Olivia thought at first it was because he was concentrating on the omelette, but then she realised Ben Chatsfield, owner of seven restaurants, could probably make an omelette in his sleep. He was hesitating because he was wondering how much to tell her. How much to share. And didn't she know how that felt. Her whole life was a closed book. She'd much rather regale people with a performance than the deficiencies of her own character, deficiencies she'd come face to face with when she'd been only twelve and her mother had been dying. Her mother who had needed her, and Olivia hadn't been able to step up to the plate. At all.

'I left home when I was eighteen,' he finally said, his back to her as he poured the egg mixture into the pan. 'Ended up in the south of France, working in the kitchen of a restaurant. The sauté chef was off sick one night and I stepped in. I took it from there.'

'From temporary sauté chef to world famous restaurateur? That was definitely the abridged version.'

He glanced over his shoulder, a smile glinting in his eyes if not quite curving his mouth. 'I suppose it was.'

'Why did you leave home?'

He turned back to the eggs, and Olivia waited. Maybe she shouldn't have asked the question; maybe that wasn't the kind of relationship, if any, that they had. But she wanted to know. She was curious about this man. Something had shifted between them tonight, from the support he'd given her at the premiere, to the kiss, to chatting over eggs. Something she liked.

'It seemed like a good idea at the time,' he finally said, and to her chagrin Olivia heard the implacable note in his voice that signalled loud and clear he did not want to talk about it any more.

'So why did you push me away tonight?' she asked instead. Better to clear the air about that one, and she'd already endured enough awkwardness not to care if there was much more. Well, not to care too much. Hopefully.

Ben added the diced vegetables to the omelette and flipped it neatly. 'You're like a dog with a bone with that one.'

'I'm a woman. I don't take rejection lightly.'

'It was hardly rejection.'

'Felt like it at the time.' She kept her voice light, slotting into her insouciant ingénue performance with ease. This was a role she knew how to play.

His mouth tightened, his eyes flashing dark. 'I told you before, I don't like the pretending element to this whole thing. It feels too much like lying. And it got to me when you kissed me in front of the crowds, just because some reporter asked you to.'

That wasn't, Olivia knew, the real reason she'd kissed him. She'd kissed him because she'd been thinking about it all night, because he'd held her hand when she'd needed him to and believed in her when it felt like no one else did. But she was not about to tell Ben Chatsfield all, or any, of that.

'That kiss didn't feel all that fake to me, Ben,' she told him with a flirty smile.

'I can hardly deny we're attracted to each other.' Hardly a compliment, yet she still felt a thrill at the simply stated fact. He slid half the omelette onto a plate which he put in front of her.

'So you were just annoyed that I obliged the reporters?' Olivia surmised. 'And kissed you to convince them we were dating?'

'I was annoyed with the whole evening. The conversation, the made-up way we met, our supposedly similar childhoods… I get that we have to do this. I know I agreed. But I don't like lying.'

Olivia picked up a fork and took a bite of omelette; it was fluffy and golden and meltingly delicious. 'Mmm. Wow. This is fantastic.'

Ben slid the other half of the omelette onto a plate and joined her at the breakfast bar. 'Thanks.'

'So let me guess,' Olivia said after she'd swallowed. 'You have a deceitful ex in your past? Some awful woman who lied to you? Cheated? That's why this little charade is getting up your nose?'

Ben's eyes flashed again and the corner of his mouth quirked slightly. 'Don't you think you're getting a little personal?'

'Well, we are supposed to be dating. We should be talking about this stuff.'

'We could talk about this stuff if we really were dating, but we're not.'

'So clearly I touched a nerve.'

He smiled then, properly, and everything in Olivia sizzled. *Whoa.* Down, girl. 'No, you didn't,' he told her. 'No deceitful exes.' He cut his omelette into several neat squares, his gaze lowered. 'If there was a deceitful person in my life,' he said after a moment, 'it was my mother.'

Now why the hell had he said that? Annoyed with himself, Ben stabbed a bit of omelette with his fork. He didn't talk about his mom, or his family, or anything. He'd been an incredibly private person since he'd left home at eighteen—which reminded him that he'd told Olivia about that too. What was going on with him?

'I'm sorry,' she said quietly, and he was surprised she didn't press. Had he sounded that bitter and angry? That sad? Honestly, he was thirty-two years old. He needed to get over all the crap that had happened when he was a kid. He *was* over it. It was just having Spencer and James back in his life, being at a Chatsfield hotel again, pretending at a relationship…all of it was raking up the old feelings. Old hurts. Old anger.

'So tell me how you got into acting,' he said, and she let out a funny little laugh.

'Well, I found out at an early age that it's nicer

being someone else than being myself.' She looked away quickly, and Ben was pretty sure she hadn't meant to admit so much. Just like he hadn't.

'Why don't you like being yourself?'

She shrugged, clearly trying to be dismissive. 'It's not so much now. But back when I was a teenager...' She shrugged again. 'I wasn't very popular in school. A few bright sparks decided to make my life miserable.' Her gaze slid away from his once more. 'Losing myself in a role was the best kind of escape.'

'I can understand that. I suppose it was similar with me and cooking. You find something you're good at and it helps with whatever life is throwing at you.'

'Yes, I think it does.' She took a breath, toying with a forkful of omelette. 'Actually, it wasn't just the bullying in school. My mother died when I was twelve and acting was my coping strategy.'

Ben felt a sharp twist of sympathy, surprising him. Olivia Harrington was making him feel things he wasn't used to feeling. Wasn't sure he should. 'I'm sorry,' he said, just as she'd said to him. She nodded jerkily.

'Thank you. It was tough but I survived.' She let out a little sigh that made Ben's insides clench with a weird kind of protectiveness. Whoa. Time to calm down inside. He clearly felt too much for this woman, for her surprising sweetness, her sudden passion, her obvious strength. Yeah, he definitely needed to pull back a little. She looked up, her eyes glinting with unshed tears as she offered him the wobbliest smile he'd ever seen. 'I still miss her, though.'

Another twist inside, and his resolution to pull back evaporated. 'Of course you do. Were you close?'

'Yes.' She nodded again, staring down at her omelette. 'Yes. Very much so.' She let out a shaky laugh and dabbed at her eyes. 'Sorry, I'm not usually this emotional. It's late and this has been a hell of a few days.' She took a deep breath and let it out slowly. 'Sorry.'

'You don't have to apologise for getting a little choked up when you talk about your mom dying, Olivia,' Ben said quietly. 'How did she die?'

'Cancer. It was actually pretty quick. A couple of months from diagnosis to...' She trailed off, shrugging. 'Well, you know.'

'Yes.'

'My father married very soon after. That was hard too. That was kind of how the bullying came about. I just didn't care any more about all the things girls that age are supposed to care about. I mouthed off to some of the cool girls and the result was they made my life hell.' Her lips tried to form what Ben suspected was meant to be a wry smile. 'Too bad they were a little late. It already was hell.'

Ben felt an aching pressure in his chest as he thought of twelve-year-old Olivia Harrington, a beauty in the making but still a little gawky and coltish, hurting so much for the mother she'd lost and the father who had found comfort elsewhere. 'I'm so sorry, Olivia,' he said quietly.

'Thanks.' She sniffed and shook her head. 'My dad died last year of a heart attack, so this is really old news.' She let out another shaky laugh. 'Honestly, I don't know why I'm telling you this. You don't need to hear my sob story.'

'Maybe you need to tell it.' She stared at him, her eyes widening in surprise, and Ben shrugged. Hell if he knew where all this was coming from. 'You don't seem like you talk about it to anyone.'

'How would you know?'

Because they were the same. He didn't talk about all his baggage either. And even though part of him now actually almost wanted to, he knew he wouldn't. 'Because you're telling me, and you seem surprised to be talking about it at all. Just like I would be, if I were talking about...' He stopped, and she cocked her head, her gaze both speculative and knowing.

'Your mom?'

'Yes.'

'What happened with her?'

He shook his head. He was not going to spill his guts, not here, not ever. He couldn't go there, couldn't get that emotional. It didn't lead to good places. Yet he also knew Olivia deserved a little honesty from him, since she'd spilled some of her secrets. 'My parents weren't all that happy together. My mother worked hard to make us look like a perfect family.' He felt his insides tighten and he took a few deep, even breaths. 'The birthday dinners in the hotel, just like you said.'

'For my tenth birthday I asked to go out for pizza,' Olivia told him with an answering smile. 'My mom agreed.'

'Sounds like she was a smart woman.'

'She was. But we were talking about your mom.'

And he didn't want to, yet somehow the words still spilled out of him. 'I wanted us to be the big happy family everyone thought we were. So I tried hard to make everyone get along, paper over the cracks, as it were. But it didn't work, and I learned it would have never worked because my mother was having an affair for most of my childhood. The whole happy-families thing was a complete lie.' He heard how his voice had risen, felt how his hands had started to clench. Damn it. He seriously needed to get a grip. 'My father had affairs too,' he continued tonelessly, 'and so I know I should be as angry at him as I've been with my mother.' Whoa, why had he mentioned the anger? 'I mean, I *was* angry. Past tense.'

'Uh-huh.' She gave him a smile so full of sympathy and understanding that the anger he was still trying to deny flared higher.

'Anyway,' he finished, his tone turning terse, 'I was a lot closer to my mother than I was to my father, and so I guess the betrayal hurt more, but I'm aware it's a bit of a double standard.'

'You can't help your feelings.'

'Sometimes, though, you should.' He slid off the bar stool and picked up their plates before taking them over to the sink. He'd spent fourteen years trying to suppress his feelings. Trying to control the rage that spurted out of him like water from a deep, boiling geyser. Yes, sometimes you definitely needed to deny your feelings.

Olivia propped her elbows on the counter, watching him. 'So this discovery,' she said, 'it happened when you were eighteen?'

He turned around, too surprised by her perception to dissemble. 'Yes...'

'And that's why you left home.'

'Nice going, Sherlock.'

'I'm quick that way.'

'Uh-huh.' He leaned against the sink and folded his arms, felt the tension spin out between them as he remembered just how she'd tasted and felt. So, so soft and silky and warm. When she'd shown up at his bedroom every thought had flown out of his head but one: how much he wanted her. And when he'd kissed her…the lid had blown off his desire. Even now he tensed to remember how desperately he'd reached for her. How mindless his need for her had been, overriding both sense and self-control. And she'd been the one to pull back. Had he been too urgent? Too *rough*?

'So now we've both kissed each other,' he said, 'both pushed each other away and both told the sob stories about our mothers. What next?'

'We could paint each other's toenails.'

He nearly laughed, enjoying her spunky comebacks. 'Tempting, but I don't have any nail varnish on me.'

'I've got some pink sparkly stuff in the other room.'

'I think I'll pass.'

'Probably a wise move.' She smiled as she eased herself off the stool, and Ben braced himself because he knew that look. It was the thanks for everything dismissal. He'd given it himself quite a few times over the years, but he found it hurt now coming from Olivia.

Which was stupid as well as pathetic. Yet he'd enjoyed his time with her, far more than he'd ever expected to. The conversation as well as the kissing. The honesty that hurt and felt good at the same time.

'It's really late, and I have a packed schedule tomorrow,' she said. 'I should get some sleep.'

He nodded and pushed off from the counter. 'Right. Me too.'

'Thanks for the omelette. It was the best one I've ever tasted.'

He shrugged her praise aside, suddenly desperate to leave—and all because he really wanted to stay so damn much. 'No problem. I'll see you... around.' He started for the door, turning around to give her one last careless wave.

'Yeah,' she said softly, and for a second she looked both sad and lost. As sad and lost as she must have been when she was twelve. Ben almost started forward—but to do what? 'Around,' she repeated, and then he went.

CHAPTER SIX

OLIVIA HAD NO time to think of Ben the next day as she raced from interview to premiere to party, and yet somehow he managed to occupy all her thoughts. The feel of his lips. The surprising sweetness of his smile. Their incredibly candid conversation, because she didn't think either of them had meant to admit so much. She'd talked about her mom dying, which, as Ben had rightly guessed, she never talked about to anyone. She had a feeling he was the same about his own mother's infidelity.

So why had they confided in each other? Had it just been a late-night type of thing, an awkward confessional over eggs? Or did they—*could* they—feel something more for each other? Something that was actually real?

Did she even want that? She'd kept herself from real or intimate relationships for a long time, and there was a reason for that. She didn't trust herself. But Olivia had to acknowledge that what she'd already experienced with Ben was weakening her resolve to stay safe and alone. She liked talking to someone. Laughing with someone. Kissing someone…

But it would be really pathetic, she told herself, to develop some kind of schoolgirl crush on her pretend boyfriend. Really stupid, because Ben wasn't giving off relationship vibes, and anyway, she had a life and a plan and Ben Chatsfield did not figure into it.

But he could…if you fell for him. If he fell for you.

If she was willing to risk her heart and try for something she'd never expected to have or even want. A terrifying prospect, but one she still found herself thinking about.

By the time she got back from the cocktail party she'd been invited to, she was utterly exhausted. She'd only had a couple of hours of sleep, and twelve hours of being on all the time had taken its toll.

She decided to take a late-night swim to clear her head and, a little voice whispered slyly, because there was an off chance she might see Ben again at the pool. Only this time she wouldn't jump on him.

Except maybe she would.

Shaking her head at her own circling thoughts, Olivia headed up to the rooftop pool, which was blissfully and just a little bit disappointingly empty at ten o'clock at night.

She swam a couple of lengths, but her heart wasn't in it and she was too tired anyway. After about twenty minutes she hauled herself up onto the side of the pool, dripping and shivering a little despite the humid, heated air. Everything was quiet save for the lap of the water against the edges of the pool, little waves she'd stirred up from her swimming. On all four sides she could see the city, endlessly dark save for the twinkling of a few lights. Suddenly Olivia felt very alone— and lonely.

It was strange to feel lonely, not to mention stupid, because she'd been alone for most of her life. Her mother's death had distanced her from her father and her siblings from one another. Everyone had orbited in their own private universe of grief. She'd been a loner in high school, only coming alive on the stage, and college had been the same. Hollywood was too cut-throat for real friends, and she'd kept herself away from the parties and gossip and affairs. Anyway, by the time she'd landed in California she'd made peace with her isolation. Besides, she had no time to feel lonely; she was too busy trying to establish and prove herself.

It was only since coming to Berlin, and meeting Ben, that she'd started feeling…unsettled. *Lonely.*

And wasn't that sad, that a couple of kisses and one semi-heartfelt conversation made her realise how isolated and empty her life really was?

Impatient with her own maudlin thoughts, she started to rise from the edge of the pool when a sharp, angry voice punctuated the silence of the pool area like the staccato fire of gunshots.

'*No*, Spencer. That is not acceptable. When I agreed to manage this hotel, I did not agree to pimp myself out.'

Olivia froze by the side of the pool. She watched the door to the men's changing room swing open hard and without thinking about what she was doing—there had, admittedly, been a lot of that lately—she dove behind a couple of stacked loungers.

Ben strode into the pool area, his cell phone clamped to his ear, his face thunderous. 'You may have no problem prostituting yourself for this damn hotel,' he snapped, 'but I do.'

Olivia went rigid with shock and mortification as the meaning of his words penetrated the numb fog of her mind. Pimp himself out. Prostitute himself for the hotel. He was talking about her. About having to pretend to date her. Pretend to like her.

She closed her eyes, shame scorching through her. She knew she shouldn't feel as humiliated and definitely not as hurt as she did. She'd known what had happened between her and Ben wasn't real.

And yet that kiss. That conversation. Those had felt real. But had he just been playing a part? And she thought she was the one with an acting career.

Ben bit off a few more terse words, and then, to Olivia's shock, he chucked the phone right at her head. No, actually, he was chucking it onto the sun lounger she was crouched behind, and it hit the soft plastic slats before sliding off and landing at her feet with a crunching kind of thud.

Oh, dear.

Ben let out a weary groan and started walking towards his phone. Olivia shrank back, but unfortunately there was nowhere left to shrink. It would be impossible for him not to see her, and that was going to make things very awkward. Again.

After a second of internal debate, she scooped up the phone and, as he came closer, she held it out to him with a smile. At least, she hoped it passed for a smile.

'I think you dropped this.'

Ben's jaw dropped and then his eyes narrowed. 'Were you…*hiding*?'

'Umm…' She scrambled up to a standing position, so at least they were eye to eye. Almost. 'No, of course not.' He eyed her sceptically and she amended, 'All right, so what if I was? It's not like I was comparing you to a—a client!'

'*What?*'

'I mean, you know…' She gestured helplessly. 'You called yourself a prostitute, so that, by association, makes me, uh, a client. Or something.' She was really starting to wish she had not started this idiotic conversation.

Ben shook his head slowly. 'You thought I was talking about you on the phone to my brother?'

She stared at him, now really disconcerted. 'Well…yes.'

His mouth tightened. 'Not everything is about you, Olivia.'

'That's a completely unfair thing to say!' she retorted, stung. 'I've never acted like everything is about me.'

'The mistake with your room?'

'Oh, you *would* bring that up again.'

To her surprise, he relaxed, or maybe deflated, and shook his head. 'No, I'm not. I can see how you'd think I'd been talking about you and our… relationship.'

Her self-righteous fury trickled away as she gazed at him. He looked tired and haggard and yet so unbearably sexy. Watching him she could remember exactly how he'd felt. How he'd tasted. She could almost imagine the slide of his lips on hers, the feel of his hands slipping under her top…

Okay. Time to stop that line of thinking. They'd already established that had been a mistake.

Although actually, now that she thought about it, they hadn't said it was a mistake. They hadn't really talked about it at all. They'd just moved on.

Sort of.

'So if you weren't talking about me, who—or rather, whom—are you pimping yourself out for?'

Ben's expression hardened, eyes flaring as he raked a hand through his hair, leaving it sticking up six ways to Sunday, and providing a painful twist to her insides. He was too sexy, too wild, too everything for his own good. And hers. 'Caris Dowling,' he said, and Olivia blinked.

'Caris Dowling, the A-list actress who gets twenty million dollars per movie?'

'That's the one, I suppose.'

Okay, the spike of jealousy she felt was totally irrational. 'So how did you snag her attention, hotshot?'

'God only knows. She's staying here and she wanted to use the lobby for her birthday party. I said no.'

'And?'

'And I thought that was it. I arranged for someone on staff to show her the various salons where we host parties, and the next thing I know Spencer is calling me claiming this Caris woman has called him a dozen times, demanding that I attend her birthday party.' He shook his head in a kind of disgusted amazement, and Olivia tilted her own, her lips twitching in amusement.

'Poor you. So Caris Dowling wants you for her newest boy toy.'

'Not a role I'm keen to fulfil.'

'She's quite good-looking…'

He grimaced. 'Not my type.'

Olivia almost asked what his type was, but fortunately she bit the question back. 'So what are you going to do?'

'Well…' Ben cocked his head, his gaze sweeping over her. 'I think that should be fairly obvious.'

'Oh?'

'It's only fair that our little arrangement has some benefit to me, don't you think?'

Olivia just waited warily, not sure where he was going with this. 'You can come with me,' Ben explained. 'The party's tomorrow night. You're my date.'

Ben adjusted the bow tie of his tux with a grimace. He hated these monkey suits, and he hated the thought of going to this blasted party just to satisfy some over-entitled movie star. The only good thing about this evening, he mused, was that he was at least going to spend it with Olivia.

And that was a very complicated good thing. He hadn't meant to kiss her the other night when she'd come to his bedroom. His brain had short-circuited at the sight of her standing there, looking so outraged and delectable and warm. And when she'd started going on about how he'd pushed her away…

Well, it had been so ludicrous, because of course he wanted her. He'd pushed her away because he'd thought that had been obvious, and that she'd only been kissing him for show.

But after the kiss—and more—in his bedroom, he was starting to reassess the situation. They were attracted to each other. They'd both admitted it. And despite their rather rocky beginning, Ben thought they actually liked each other. They'd had a surprisingly honest conversation over omelettes, and while that kind of honesty could be unsettling and uncomfortable, it had also been strangely good. Maybe even needed. And he was realising he and Olivia were more like each other than he ever would have expected.

So where was he going with this? Because their relationship was still definitely in the pretend-only realm, and that was the way Ben wanted it. He didn't have room in his life or his heart for anything else. He didn't trust himself enough to handle an actual, real relationship.

The anger was still too present. Olivia had seen it in little things, the way he'd lost his temper with her in the pool or with Spencer on the phone. He hated that she'd seen it, hated what it revealed in himself.

He'd kept his anger under control for fourteen years, but coming back to The Chatsfield had been like prying open the lid on the Pandora's box of his emotions. He hated how much he'd felt since walking these halls, dredging up old memories of the family he'd tried to please, the boy he'd been.

Attempting some kind of relationship, even a casual fling, with Olivia was way too complicated for him to think about now.

He headed up to her suite, rolling his shoulders in a useless attempt to dislodge the knot of tension that had settled between them. He knocked on the door and the breath dried in his throat as he gaped at Olivia for a moment.

She looked stunning. She always looked stunning, perfectly coiffed and made-up and glamorous, but the emerald full-length gown she wore now took her beauty to a whole new level. The vivid colour brought out the glints in her eyes and hair, and moulded to her body in a way that left just enough to the imagination. High, firm breasts. Tiny waist. Endless legs.

Eventually his gaze made it back to her face and he saw she was grinning mischievously. 'Finished?'

'Almost,' he answered, and just for the hell of it,

he let his gaze go walkabout again. She laughed, shaking her head, her hands on her hips, which showcased her breasts even better.

They were definitely flirting, and this time they didn't have an audience. Their relationship, Ben acknowledged, had just gone up a notch. The conversation and the kiss had changed things between them. They weren't, he knew, pretending so much any more, and he didn't know how he felt about that.

'You look fantastic,' he said, and she tossed her head in what was, he realised with a jolt, a perfect imitation of Caris Dowling.

'Thank you, darling. But there's really no need to state the obvious.'

He laughed, impressed by her drawled vowels and sexy pout, both all too reminiscent of the entitled star. 'Clearly you have a gift for mimicry.'

She upped the pout. 'I have many gifts, sweetie.'

'That woman is seriously a horror.'

'She's won awards though.' She dropped the act, shaking her head at him. 'How did a surly chef end up playing host to a bunch of overindulged celebs?'

'I'm either a sucker or a nice guy.' Or just a brother who was still too eager to please.

'Hmm. You don't strike me as either.' She frowned speculatively, and Ben resisted tugging at his too-tight collar. He didn't need any analysis tonight, and certainly not about the difficult dynamics between him and Spencer.

'Come on. We don't want to be late for this thing.'

'Anyone who is anyone is late to these things.'

'But if we show up on time, we can leave early.' Too late he realised that sounded like some kind of intent on his part. *If we leave early, we can go do something by ourselves...like finish what we started the other night.*

Except he wasn't sure Olivia even wanted to finish it. She'd been the one to call time, after all. Of course, he had been moving a little fast. With a rush of both longing and recrimination, he remembered how good she'd felt. How much he'd wanted her. And how little self-control he really possessed.

'So where is this party?' Olivia asked, thankfully interrupting his thoughts.

'In the Parisian Salon.'

'And is Caris Dowling going to be annoyed when you show up with me on your arm?'

Ben shrugged. 'Probably.'

'This isn't going to be good for my career, you know,' Olivia said with a shake of her head. 'Showing up one of the most powerful women in Hollywood.'

'And showing everyone else that you're the next big thing,' Ben countered. 'Besides, I think I'm more of a temporary amusement for Ms Dowling. She'll forget about me by morning.'

'She will if I have anything to do with it,' Olivia promised, her eyes sparkling, and Ben felt his mouth kick up in a smile.

'You aren't going to do anything crazy, are you?'

Olivia rounded her eyes innocently. 'Who? Me? When do I ever do anything that isn't carefully thought out?'

'This should be interesting,' Ben murmured, and they stepped into the salon.

Caris zeroed in on him almost instantly. Ben tensed as she moved towards him, arms outstretched, a half-full glass of champagne dangling dangerously from her manicured fingers.

'Caris!' Olivia's voice was like the peal of a crystal bell. She started forward, hands outstretched, and did the Hollywood kiss-kiss thing on both cheeks. Ben knew he should be used to it; he lived in France after all. But the sight of two women bussing each other's cheeks even as at least one of them had eyes that shot daggers was…

Funny.

For once he could see the funny side of this kind of pretending. He felt his tension drain away as he watched Olivia's mouth turn up in a high beam of a smile. He was going to enjoy this, he decided as she chatted Caris's ear off before turning to Ben with a tug on his fingers. 'Ben, darling? Isn't it *so* funny that you and Caris are friends? *Such* a small world.' She turned back to Caris with that full-wattage smile and Ben had to suppress a laugh.

Caris, poor woman, could do nothing but nod stiffly. She wasn't going to lose face at her own party, not in front of an actress who was, Ben knew, younger and more beautiful than she was.

Olivia had her nailed.

After a few pained moments of chit-chat Caris excused herself. Olivia plucked a glass of champagne from a tray and watched her disappear through the crowds with satisfaction.

'I don't think she'll bother you again.'

'I wasn't aware I needed rescuing,' Ben answered dryly, and Olivia turned to him with a devilish glint in her eyes.

'Oh, can girls not charge to the rescue in your world?'

'Actually,' Ben said, stepping closer to her, 'you were magnificent. Caris Dowling didn't stand a chance.'

Olivia's eyes widened at this bit of praise, and then her mouth curved up in that teasing smile Ben was really starting to like. He'd dismissed Olivia as shallow, but now that he knew of the depths she had to her, he could appreciate her sense of humour and fun.

'She didn't, did she?' she agreed, her eyes sparkling. 'Unfortunately I've just made an enemy of one of the most powerful women in Hollywood.'

'Her star's on the wane, if you ask me. And yours is on the rise.'

'Let's hope so.' Olivia made a face, but Ben could tell she was enjoying herself…just as he was enjoying himself.

Too much, maybe.

Now that Caris had left them alone, there was no reason to stay. Normally Ben would have been happy to bow out, swim a few dozen laps and hit the sack. Now, however, he had a gorgeous woman on his arm, a glass of champagne in his hand, and for the first time in years he actually wanted to enjoy himself. With Olivia.

'Care to dance?' he asked, and her eyes widened some more. Her smile kicked up. She deposited her half-drunk glass on a passing tray.

'I thought you'd never ask.'

This was dangerous, Olivia knew as she glided in Ben's arms on the salon's dance floor. Dangerous and very, very nice. A string orchestra had just struck up a tune and Ben slid his hands around her waist, his fingers dipping down towards her butt. Shivers of pleasure rippled through her and she tilted her head to smile up at him.

'I didn't take you for a dancer.'

'I'm not usually. But it seemed a shame not to, considering the circumstances.'

'Which are?'

'The music. The party. Your dress.'

Something fluttered low in her belly. 'You like this dress, huh?'

He pulled her closer, so her hips and thighs came into exquisite contact with his. 'I love this dress,' he murmured in her ear, and this time Olivia shivered for real.

What were they doing? One minute it was all banter and flirt as they pretended for the public, and the next it felt all too real. All too intense.

And Olivia didn't know which she wanted. No, she knew what she wanted. Wanted very, very badly. She was just afraid to want it…for a whole lot of reasons.

Ben tightened his hold on her and after a second's hesitation she rested her cheek against his shoulder. It was easier than trying to angle her head away from him, and the truth was she'd been wanting to do it since he'd first taken her in his arms. He felt hard and safe and comforting all at once, and his throat was so close she could lick it.

Not that she was going to do something that

stupid and frankly weird. She'd just think about it for a little while.

The music ebbed and swelled in a tide of sound and they swayed to its languorous beat, Ben's hands tightening on her hips as Olivia nestled against him. She never wanted the moment to end, never wanted to stop breathing in the clean, male scent of him, of feeling his arms around her. Of feeling safe and cherished and loved.

Ridiculous, of course, to feel all that. She *knew* that. They were little more than strangers. And yet she'd shared more of herself with Ben than with anyone else in just about ever. She felt more for him than she had any other man. She didn't move.

Eventually the music ended and couples began to leave the dance floor. Neither of them moved for a moment, just kept swaying to the music that was no longer playing. Then Ben eased back, and when Olivia risked a look upwards she saw that his expression was fiercely intent, almost primal, his eyes blazing, and her heart lurched against her ribs. Then it started beating double time as Ben took her hand in his own, lacing their fingers together, and without so much as a word led her off the dance floor and out of the ballroom.

CHAPTER SEVEN

AT SOME POINT between taking her in his arms to dance and leading her off the floor, Ben had decided to ignore all his intentions and principles. He wanted Olivia. She wanted him. This could, he decided, be simple. He'd cautioned himself against a fling, but he was tired of caution. Tired of denying himself. In little more than a week they'd never see each other again. Why not explore and enjoy this attraction?

And the truth was, he didn't have the will power or self-control not to.

Olivia didn't resist, didn't so much as offer a single question, as he led her away from the party, through the hotel lobby and then into the lift that led to the floor of executive suites.

As the lift moved upwards Ben turned to her. Her eyes were huge, her lips parted, her breath coming out in a rush as he pressed her against the wall and kissed her with all the pent-up need and desire he felt. Blood roared in his ears and his libido took over. He grabbed handfuls of slippery satin as he yanked her dress upwards, needing to feel her bare flesh against his. His hand found the smooth, warm skin of her calf and he groaned aloud as he slid it upwards to her thigh.

Olivia's head fell back, her breath coming in shallow pants.

'Too much dress,' he muttered, and she let out a wild laugh that fired his blood even more.

The doors pinged open.

Ben stepped back, the need pulsing through him so hard and fast his vision blurred. Wordlessly he turned from Olivia and left the elevator. She followed, fumbling for her key card in her clutch.

She was taking too long with it, and Ben needed to feel her against him again. He turned to her, framing her face with his palms, his fingers sliding through her luxuriant hair. She tilted her face upwards, waiting for and silently inviting his kiss, her clutch dangling uselessly from her fingers.

He kissed her slowly this time, trying to pace himself, letting his whole body absorb the sweet softness of her yielding mouth.

Her hands came up to cling to the lapels of his tux, her body arching closer to his as their tongues twined together. Lust bit with deep urgency and Ben pressed her against the door, not caring if anyone saw them. Not caring about anything or anyone but her.

He slid his hand down the slippery smooth material of her dress, cupped the ripe fullness of her breast and ran his thumb over the taut peak. Heard Olivia let out a little mewl of sound, and satisfaction roared inside him, along with an even deeper need.

And then he felt her hands flatten against his chest, and she pressed lightly, turning her head away from his. Ben felt as if he'd been dipped in ice water. Once again Olivia was retreating, and suddenly he realised he had no idea if he'd been mauling her for the past few minutes, or if it had been mutual. He'd been too overwhelmed to think clearly, or at all.

He stepped back, shame scorching through him as he realised how aggressive and urgent he'd been. 'Olivia…'

She let out a shaky laugh. 'You're a wonderful kisser, you know…'

'Yet you stopped.'

'Yes.' She took a deep breath, as if she were going to say something more, but then she let out a sigh, twisting out of his embrace and fumbling to retrieve her key card from her clutch. 'Do you want to come in for a drink?'

Warily Ben watched her, wondered just what was going through her mind. 'All right.'

She swiped the key card and he followed her into the luxurious suite. He could tell she seemed nervous, although she was trying not to be. She tossed her clutch onto the hall table and then went into the kitchen, searching in the fridge he'd stocked himself for something to drink.

'There's a bottle of white wine on the bottom shelf,' he said, propping one shoulder against the doorway, and she turned around to give him a quick, distracted smile.

'Great.'

'Shall I open it?'

'Would you?' She thrust the bottle at him and Ben took it, moving past her to retrieve a corkscrew from one of the kitchen drawers. He twisted it in and popped the cork neatly, pouring them both glasses and handing one to her. 'What's going on, Olivia?' he asked quietly.

Her knuckles were white as she clutched her glass. 'What do you mean?'

'You're freaking out,' he stated, and then forced himself to ask, 'Did I scare you?'

'*Scare* me?' She blinked at him in surprise. 'No.'

'Then why did you kiss me like you meant it, and then back away? I think we both knew where this was going. What we want.' He swallowed, because the truth was, he wasn't sure he did know if they wanted the same thing. And he wanted it very badly. 'Don't we?'

Olivia took a rather large swig of wine before meeting his gaze with what felt like reluctance. Her face was nearly crimson. She was, Ben realised in surprise, blushing. 'We do,' she said, her voice little more than a whisper. She cleared her throat. 'That is…maybe you should clarify what you want.'

'You,' Ben answered bluntly. He felt too much raw need for her to prevaricate now. 'You in bed now, although to be frank it doesn't have to be on a bed. Just about anywhere would be fine.'

She gulped, her eyes flaring, and Ben took a step towards her. 'I want you. A lot. But if you're not on board with it, then tell me now.'

'I…' She licked her lips and Ben nearly groaned aloud. 'I'm on board with it,' she whispered. 'That is…if you're talking about just sex. A fling.'

'Yes. I'm not interested in a serious relationship.'

'I'm not either.'

Which made him want to ask why, but he wasn't going to go there now. There was only one place he wanted to go right now.

'So we're on the same page here,' he remarked, 'but you've still got a death grip on that glass.'

'It's just…' Olivia let out a shaky laugh. 'This is kind of awkward.'

'It doesn't need to be.'

'Yes, well, that's because you don't know…' She trailed off, took another sip of wine.

Ben tensed. 'I don't know what?'

She took a deep breath and let it out slowly. 'This is the awkward part.' She walked into the living area and flopped down on the white leather sofa, her dress spreading around her in bright emerald-green folds. She looked like a mermaid afloat in an ocean of leather. She stared at him, her chin raised defiantly. 'The truth is, I haven't done this before.'

'What?' He stared at her, nonplussed. She hadn't had a casual fling before? He was surprised; she'd seemed pretty savvy and sexually confident.

Olivia's mouth twisted mockingly. 'I don't mean that I haven't had a fling or a one-night stand before,' she elaborated, 'since that is obviously what you've just assumed. I mean…I haven't…' She bit her lip and then let out another gusty breath. 'I've never had sex.'

Ben just stared. And stared. Olivia felt her face flush again and her insides curl up into a self-protective ball of humiliation. *The look on his face.* She might as well have said she had some terrible disease.

'That's unexpected,' he finally said, his voice toneless, and Olivia wished she could have taken that awful, awkward confessional back. Why on earth had she admitted it anyway? She was an actress after all. She could have faked some sexual experience. Ben might never have known.

That was assuming they ended up sleeping together. Which at this point, judging by Ben's carefully blank look, seemed pretty unlikely. Maybe he didn't sleep with virgins.

'It just…never happened,' she explained, and Ben arched an eyebrow.

'No? I'm surprised.'

'Of course there have been opportunities,' Olivia huffed before she could stop herself. 'I mean, if I'd really wanted to turn in my V-card I could have done it, easily. It's not *that*.'

'No, of course not.'

'Let's just stop talking about this,' she muttered. She downed the rest of her wine and then rose from the sofa. 'Where's the bottle?'

'I'm not sure alcohol will help the situation, but I left it in the kitchen.'

She stalked towards the kitchen and topped up her glass right to the brim. 'And just what is the *situation*, Ben?' she asked, a rather nasty note entering her voice. She didn't want his pity. She didn't want him laughing at her either. She just wanted…

Him. Yes, she still wanted him. Despite the awkwardness, the embarrassment, she wanted him. Badly. Enough to have admitted her inexperience.

Ben had followed her into the kitchen and he stood in the doorway, watching her as she glugged more wine.

'Easy there, killer.'

She glared at him over the rim of her glass. 'I'm fine.'

'You're more than fine, Olivia. You're beautiful and smart and talented and sexy as hell. If I'm surprised you haven't had sex before, it's just because you're so amazing.'

Olivia's jaw nearly dropped at his words—and his tone. Heartfelt sincerity. She'd never heard it from him, and she could tell by the slightly startled look in his eyes that he hadn't expected to say all that. But she knew he meant it.

'Oh.' She put her wine glass on the granite counter with a loud clunk. 'Well. Thank you.'

'You're welcome.'

'You didn't think any of that when you first met me,' she felt compelled to point out.

'True. I didn't know you then. Things have changed.'

Had they changed that much? He wanted to sleep with her, but that was all. No point getting ahead of herself and going mushy over a few compliments. And in any case, maybe he didn't want to sleep with her any more. She didn't really feel like asking. She took another sip of wine.

'So there were opportunities,' Ben asked. 'But no takers?'

'I didn't want it to be with just anybody,' Olivia answered with a shrug, and then realised what she was implying about her and Ben. 'I mean, I was never waiting for true love or something like that,' she said quickly. 'I just didn't fancy it with anyone when I was younger. High school was pretty much a write-off, and in college I focused on acting. Then I was older and it felt awkward, explaining…' She sighed. 'About as awkward as this is.'

'There's no need to feel awkward, Olivia. You've been discerning. That's a good thing.'

'You think?' she asked wryly. 'Sometimes I wish I'd just had done with it.'

He took a step towards her, that need she'd felt from him earlier emanating from him, blazing in his eyes. 'And now?' he asked in a low voice. 'Do you want me the way I want you?'

'Yes,' she whispered. She couldn't deny it, didn't want to. 'I do. I want…I want my first time to be with you.'

Heat flared in his eyes even as he shook his head, making Olivia's hopes free-fall. 'I meant what I said. I don't do relationships. This will only be a fling, Olivia. A couple of weeks, max.'

'That's what I want. Just because I'm a virgin doesn't mean I'm angling for a wedding ring,

Ben.' She kept her voice tart because his warning had hurt just a little, even if she understood it. Agreed with it.

Sort of.

'Good.'

'I want to stay focused on my career right now,' she said firmly. 'And have some amazing sex. So do you think you can oblige?'

Ben's mouth quirked up in a smile. 'I think I can, as long as you understand…'

'Enough with the warnings,' she cut across him. 'You're not going to break my heart, okay?' At least, she hoped he wasn't. Because she wasn't at all sure she believed what she'd just said.

'Good.'

'So…' She held out her arms, half expecting him to reach for her and head for the bedroom. 'What now?'

Ben rubbed his jaw thoughtfully. 'Well, I can't pretend this doesn't change things a little.'

'It doesn't have to…'

'I'm not going to make love with you tonight.'

Make love. Words that sent a shivery thrill running through her, even as disappointment followed in its wake as his meaning registered. 'Why not?'

'Because a first time ought to be special.'

'Oh, please.' She rolled her eyes. 'I'm not sixteen and in search of hearts and roses. Besides, I bet most women's first times aren't special at all.

They're probably in the back of a car or a cheap hotel room after prom.'

'Maybe I want this to be special.'

Olivia nearly guffawed. 'Yeah, right.'

He looked intent in a whole different way then. 'Seriously, Olivia. Why shouldn't it be? Remember what I said about the limo?'

'If we're going to do it, do it right?'

'Exactly.'

'And I suppose you mean that literally now.'

'Of course.'

She took a deep breath, plunged. 'Fine. When, then?'

'You free tomorrow night?'

'For sex? I suppose.'

'Good.' He reached for her then, tugging on her hands, drawing her to him. She came slowly, a little reluctantly, because this all felt so strange and yet also oddly right. He framed her face with his hands, tucking a stray tendril of hair behind her ear, his touch so tender that Olivia felt tears sting her eyes. She hadn't expected that. 'I'll pick you up at seven,' he said, and kissed her.

It was a soft, sweet kiss, a gentle kiss, a kiss of promise rather than intent. 'See you tomorrow,' he whispered against her lips, and then he was gone.

Olivia Harrington was a virgin. So not what he'd been expecting from that conversation. Ben shook his head in bemused disbelief. He never would have guessed it in a million years, which just showed what a good actress she really was. Since the moment he'd met her she had projected an air of saucy, sexual experience. Not complete innocence.

And yet he couldn't condemn her for being fake, at least not in that regard. No, if anything, he saw it as bravery. It was hard to be something you didn't always feel inside. He knew that all too well.

Olivia might be hiding her inexperience and nervousness, but he was hiding something far more dangerous. His anger. The kind of rage that had nearly killed a man. And he was afraid, with his emotions scraped so raw, he wouldn't have as tight a rein on his emotion as he normally did. Hell, he already knew he didn't.

But that had nothing to do with him and Olivia.

He suffered a moment's hesitation at taking Olivia's virginity, but then he shrugged it aside. She was twenty-six years old and she wanted to have sex. He wanted to be the man to show her. And when it came to their time together, he'd make sure it was as sweet and gentle and wonderful as he could make it.

CHAPTER EIGHT

WHAT TO WEAR for your first time? Underwear clearly was key, and Olivia had raced out to the Galeries Lafayette in Berlin to purchase some high-end lingerie. She'd roved through the racks of silk and satin, spending far too much time debating her choice. Nothing too racy or debauched, she decided as she moved past the black lace bustiers and the fire-engine-red see-through push-up bra and thong. Such get-ups would just make her look like she was trying too hard to be something Ben now knew very well she was not.

For the same reason she decided against the modest white lace negligees and demure nighties. No need to state the obvious either.

Which left her with very few options unfortunately.

'Looking for something special?' A saleswoman coasted up to her and Olivia suppressed a groan. Yes, as a matter of fact, she was, but she didn't feel like admitting it to this woman—or to anyone.

The first time should be special, Ben had said. Olivia supposed she should agree with him in theory, but she felt the expectation weigh on her heavily now. What if it wasn't special? What if she messed up somehow, or said or did something embarrassing? What if she wasn't good enough for Ben in some inexplicable way?

Because while she'd admitted she hadn't had sex, she hadn't been all that forthcoming about how little experience she truly had. A couple of kisses, that was all. She hadn't let it bother her before; she was too focused. Now she felt her ignorance like a weight on her back, on her soul. Yes, she'd seen plenty of movies, read romance novels, had fantasies like any other normal woman. Of course she had. But it wasn't the same as actually…

'Are you sure you're all right?' the woman asked, and Olivia gave her a sickly sweet smile.

'Perfect,' she said, and grabbed the first bra her hand reached for off the rack.

Fifteen minutes later she left the shop with a plain black silk bra and matching pants. Nothing particularly romantic or sexy about either of them, and she had an equivalent pair back in her suite. If she'd been trying to accomplish something with her underwear purchase, she'd failed.

Back at her suite she tossed the bag onto a chair and ran a bath. Ben was picking her up in just under two hours, and already her stomach was writhing as if she'd swallowed snakes. Her hands shook as she emptied the bubble bath into the tub. Good grief, she needed to get a *grip*.

She'd managed, by sheer force of will, to calm herself a little by the time she was dressed and waiting for Ben to pick her up. She wore the black underwear she'd bought, because at least it was new, and a plain black shift dress that had tiny bits of diamante sewn into the gauzy fabric, so she sparkled when she moved. Understated, elegant, sophisticated. She hoped.

The doorbell rang and Olivia resisted the urge to wipe her damp palms down the sides of her dress. She took a deep breath, put a breezy smile on her face. *Showtime*.

'Well, hello there.' She let her smile turn flirty as she took in his outfit: a black button-down shirt open at the throat and grey trousers. Very sexy.

'You look lovely.' Ben leaned in to kiss her cheek, and Olivia closed her eyes as she breathed in the clean, woodsy scent of him. 'You haven't changed your mind?' he murmured as he eased back, and her eyes flew open.

'No.'

'Good.'

'Where are we going?'

'We're staying at The Chatsfield.'

'Okay.'

He turned to her with a smile as they waited for the elevator. 'Have you eaten in the restaurant before?'

'Nope.'

'First time for everything,' he teased, and she shook her head, caught between amusement and embarrassment.

'Those kinds of jokes are going to get really old, really fast.'

'Yeah, I know. I'll stop.'

Yet she liked this lighter side to Ben, Olivia decided as they stepped into the elevator and it soared upwards. She liked seeing him look happy and relaxed, because so often he didn't. So often, she realised, he seemed taut with the tension of reining things in. Keeping himself under control.

She hoped he'd let go tonight.

The Chatsfield's restaurant was on the floor below the pool, with a panoramic view of the city. It was exclusive and upmarket, just like the hotel, and nervously she wondered how she'd get through a three-course meal with Ben, all the while thinking about what was going to happen after.

'Relax,' Ben murmured, and she turned to him with a frown.

'I'm not nervous.'

'You're not that good an actress, Olivia.'

'Shut up.'

He just chuckled, and she found herself smiling, and somehow her nervousness trickled away. It was going to be okay. Maybe even great. Why not have high expectations?

The doors pinged open and Ben ushered her forward, one warm hand on her lower back.

Olivia stepped into the restaurant, blinking as she took in the empty tables glimmering under candlelight.

'Where is everyone?'

'I closed the restaurant.'

'You—what?'

'I closed the restaurant,' he repeated easily. 'Manager's privileges. Anyway, the staff needed a break. They've been working hard catering to all these celebrities.'

Olivia gazed around the sea of tables, the room flickering with shadows cast from the candles on every one. Outside the lights of the city twinkled under an ebony sky. She took a deep breath, let it out slowly.

'That's quite a privilege. This restaurant is usually fully booked.' And there had to be at least a dozen high-profile Hollywood types who were annoyed at having their reservations cancelled.

'You're worth it,' he told her, and guided her to a chair at a table in the centre of the restaurant, by a window that overlooked the Tiergarten.

'Technically,' she answered, 'you don't know that.'

'You think I have any doubts?' Ben asked, one eyebrow arched in amused disbelief. 'A single kiss has kept me awake all night. I'm not worried, Olivia. And you shouldn't be either.'

Colour touched her cheekbones and she reached for her napkin. 'Fine…'

'Now, now, let me.' Smiling he took the heavy linen napkin from her and spread it in her lap, letting his hands linger on her thighs. Sparks leaped in Olivia's belly. She nearly shuddered.

Okay, she wasn't really worried. They had chemistry, definitely. But it still felt new and strange—and exciting.

Very exciting.

'So what's on the menu?' she asked lightly. 'Besides me, of course.'

'Nothing nearly as delicious as that,' Ben answered, his lips twitching in a smile, 'but I'll do my best.'

She glanced around the empty restaurant once more. 'No wait staff?'

'I gave them the night off.'

'I hope they appreciated it.'

'Considering they were fully paid, I think so.'

She swallowed. Audibly. 'You've gone to an awful lot of effort, Ben.'

'I wanted to,' he said simply. His gaze was warm

and steady and made Olivia swallow again. He wanted to...for her. When had anyone wanted to do anything for her? She'd been the one always striving and trying so hard to prove herself. Now she thought she might like to be pampered. Spoiled. Because she was worth it.

Except you know you actually aren't.

She pushed that treacherous little voice away and smiled at Ben. 'Thank you,' she said, and he smiled back.

'You're welcome. And now I need to get the first course.'

She sat back, trying to let herself relax and enjoy the beautiful, luxurious surroundings as Ben fetched their first courses from their kitchen. She wondered what he'd serve her. Oysters on crushed ice? Not that she actually needed an aphrodisiac. Her whole body was buzzing with both adrenalin and expectation.

He returned a few minutes later with two plates of paper-thin beef carpaccio artfully arranged amidst sprigs of thyme and drizzled with olive oil.

'I kept it simple,' he told her as he laid the plates on the table. 'Had more important things on my mind.'

'Do you mean you cooked for me?' Olivia asked, and Ben gave a self-deprecating smile and shrug in reply.

'I thought someone in the kitchen might spoil the mood.'

'It looks delicious.' She felt both touched and humbled by how much effort he'd gone to. The restaurant was awash in candlelight, the food and wine beyond delicious. And Ben himself... he looked serious and intent and rumpled and gorgeous. In other words, perfect.

Olivia knew, with a heartrending certainty, she'd never forget this night. She'd never want to. The thought brought a lump to her throat. As far as flings went, this was already off the charts in terms of her emotional investment...which was more than a little scary.

'You Chatsfields certainly know how to make a girl feel special,' she said teasingly, and a tiny frown appeared between Ben's eyebrows.

'Us Chatsfields?'

'Surely you didn't fail to notice the huge billboard James took out in Times Square when he proposed to Princess Leila?' Not, she realised belatedly, that she wanted to be making that comparison. 'Were you close to your brothers?' she continued quickly, desperate to get the conversation on a different track. 'Spencer and James?'

'I know their names.' Ben's gaze roved over her, mouth tightening. So, a sensitive subject apparently. 'Yes, we were, actually, very close.' He lowered his gaze, the candlelight casting his face into planes of light and shadow. 'We called ourselves the Three Musketeers.'

'And which one were you? I admit, I haven't read the book, but I'm familiar with the film version.' She smiled, wanting to dispel a little of the darkness she saw in his eyes. 'Were you Athos? Aramis? I can't remember the name of the third one, the one who was a dandy…'

'Porthos,' Ben filled in with a faint smile. 'I don't know which one I was.' He paused, his long, lean fingers toying with his fork as a frown furrowed his forehead. 'If one of them was a peacemaker,' he said slowly, 'that was me.'

'A peacemaker,' Olivia repeated thoughtfully, fascinated by this sudden insight into Ben's childhood. 'Were there many arguments?'

'My parents argued a lot, even though they pretended that they didn't. And my father argued a lot with Spencer.'

'Why Spencer?'

Ben pressed his lips together. 'They just didn't get along.'

'And so you tried to intervene? Keep the peace?'

'As much as I could. I don't think I was very successful. But yes, I tried.'

She could imagine him, a young boy desperate to keep everyone happy and never quite able to manage it. She wondered if that was why he had that wildness in him now…because he'd always had to be the stable, sane one who kept every-one else on an even keel. Maybe he'd never had a chance to truly let go.

And maybe he would with her tonight.

Ben raised his gaze to hers. 'What about you? Were you close to someone in particular, one of your sisters?'

'Not really,' Olivia admitted with a frown. 'We all had our own interests, I suppose. I wish we were closer sometimes.' She hesitated, then added impulsively, 'I was close to my mother, though, more so than my siblings. We were very similar. Both of us had a flair for the dramatic.'

'Is that why you went into acting?'

'Yes.' More than he could ever know…than she'd ever tell him. 'I know she'd be glad that I did.'

'Being so close, it must have made it very hard when she died.'

'Yes.' Olivia felt that familiar burning in her chest. She suppressed the urge to press her hand to her chest, as if that would alleviate the pain. Nothing would. She'd lived with the loss of her mother, and her own failure in that regard, for fourteen years already. She didn't think it would ever go away.

'This conversation's become rather serious all of a sudden,' she said in as light a tone as she could manage. 'Maybe we should talk about something else.'

'How about the second course?' Ben suggested. 'And you can tell me all about this film you're hoping to get a role in.'

He disappeared again, and Olivia took the opportunity to compose herself. She shouldn't have mentioned her mother, yet for some reason when she spent time with Ben she started *saying* things. He was a good listener, but more importantly, he seemed to actually care about what she said. What she felt. It was an unusual feeling, and she had to admit she liked it. Liked feeling important to someone.

Whoa. Don't get ahead of yourself. Fling, remember?

Yeah. Fling.

'So this film,' Ben said when he'd returned with two steaming plates. He put one in front of Olivia and she inhaled the delicious aroma of orange and lime. 'Wild salmon steaks with citrus *beurre blanc*,' Ben explained. 'A bistro speciality.'

'It looks and smells amazing.'

'So tell me about this film.'

'Well.' She took a bite of the salmon, the flavours bursting and then melting on her tongue, as she marshalled her thoughts. 'It's a war drama, and I'm up for the lead role, the wife of a missing marine. My first lead in a major film.'

'And when will you find out if it's yours?'

Just thinking about this role made her nerves start to jangle. 'Hopefully by the end of the festival. The producers wanted to see how my role in *Blue Skies Forever* went over, but they told my agent it's a done deal. Well, nearly.'

'And so you can't afford for anything to mess it up,' Ben surmised softly, and she let out a self-conscious laugh.

'You mean our dating debacle, I suppose.'

'I don't know how much of a debacle it's turned out to be,' Ben answered, and Olivia felt a thrill rise up in her like a wave, crashing over her senses. So this was what it felt like to be wanted. Desired. *Treasured.*

Ben's steady, approving gaze was the most powerful aphrodisiac in the world. Her throat tightened and she licked her lips before saying, 'Ben…all the trouble you've taken tonight with the food, the restaurant…I really appreciate it. This has been the most incredible night of my life so far.' She blushed at this admission, but Ben just smiled.

'And we haven't even got started.'

'No, we haven't.' Olivia murmured her agreement, her mind dancing with images of just what getting started would look like. Feel like.

'I love it when you blush,' Ben told her, his voice a low, sexy rumble that stole right through her. 'It makes me wonder if you blush all over.'

Heat scorched through her and she shifted in her seat, amazed at how quickly and easily he'd been able to ramp up the desire in her.

'But first,' he continued, a hint of laughter in his voice, 'dessert.'

He cleared their plates and after he'd disappeared into the kitchen, Olivia rose from the table, too restless to sit still any longer. Her whole body pulsed with expectation; she felt too alive and excited to feel any fear or nervousness now.

Soon…soon Ben would touch her. Kiss her with that wildness she remembered, the unrestrained urgency that thrilled her to her core. Soon she would know what it was like to be possessed by him completely…

She paced the elegant confines of the restaurant, the city spread out in a map of twinkling lights all around her. Where was Ben? He'd been gone for ten minutes at least, and each minute had stretched on endlessly as she waited. Waited and wanted…

But why should she wait a moment longer? She might be inexperienced, but that didn't mean she had to be shy. Turning on her heel, desire firing her resolve, Olivia made her way to the kitchen.

Ben stared at the boiling mess with exasperation. Okay, maybe chocolate fondue hadn't been the best choice for dessert. He'd wanted something romantic and sensual, but he also hadn't wanted to be a slave to the kitchen. So he'd put the chocolate on a double boiler to melt with the cream on low heat while he and Olivia had eaten their main course.

And ended up with a boiling, frothing fondue because he hadn't paid attention to the time. He'd been too busy enjoying himself, revelling in the time he'd spent with Olivia—and the knowledge of the time they'd have later. Watching her eat, seeing how her throat worked as she sipped her wine, even just the way she'd held her fork…all of it had been the most exquisite form of torture.

But now dessert was nearly ruined. Quickly he tossed in a knob of butter and a little water to smooth out the fondue. He whisked briskly, wondering what Olivia was thinking as she waited by herself in the restaurant. Wishing he hadn't been quite so clever in deciding to cook for her, but cooking was the best way he knew of showing someone he cared.

And do you care about Olivia?

'Ben?'

He looked up, saw her standing amidst the hanging pots and stainless-steel counters. She gave him one of her playful smiles, a hint of vulnerability in her eyes, and his chest—his whole body—ached with longing.

'Sorry. Slight dessert emergency.'

She came forward, her hips swaying, the glittery fabric of her dress moulding to her breasts. 'What happened?'

'The fondue boiled over. I'm afraid the company was just too scintillating and I forgot about it.'

She gave him a mischievous look and then dipped her finger into the chocolate, bringing it to her lips and then slowly licking it off. *Sweet heaven.*

'Tastes all right to me,' she said, and he nearly dropped the whisk. Dropped everything so he could take her in his arms and kiss the chocolate from her mouth.

'There are strawberries and pineapple to go with it,' he said, his voice coming out a little hoarse.

'Strawberries?' Olivia's mouth curved in invitation. Ben could see a little dab of chocolate on the corner of her mouth and he suppressed the very deep and primal urge to lick it off.

'Yes…'

She reached forward, giving him a fantastic view of her cleavage, and took a strawberry from the bowl he'd put out. She dipped it in the chocolate and then slowly, languorously, licked it off. Ben groaned aloud.

'Olivia…you're killing me here.'

She raised her eyebrows. 'Then you must be on a suicide mission. Why don't you come over here and put us both out of our misery?'

He hesitated, not because he didn't want to, because God knew he did, more than anything else, but because he'd had a plan. Dessert and a build-up of desire and expectation, and then he'd take her back to her suite and make love to her slowly, sweetly. He'd keep it gentle and safe, which was what a woman's first time needed to be. What he needed it to be.

'Ben.' She put her hands on her hips, shook her hair back as she levelled him with a look of pure, insistent desire. 'Kiss me.'

He couldn't say no to that. One kiss, and then they'd go back to her suite with the candles and the rose petals and the romance. One little kiss.

He tossed the whisk aside and took her in his arms, brushing his mouth against hers. She tasted of strawberries and chocolate and he couldn't get enough. He kissed her again, deeper this time, sliding his tongue into the softness of her mouth as a groan of pure longing escaped him and the need overtook him, banishing any resolutions he'd had.

Her arms twined around his neck and she

pressed her body against him so he could feel the softness of her breasts, the sweet juncture of her thighs. He groaned again, his fingers itching to slide under the slippery material of her dress, to feel the satin of her skin against his palms…

'We should stop.' He tried to ease away but she wouldn't let him.

'Stop? I didn't think that word was in our vocabulary tonight.'

'We're in the kitchen, Olivia…'

'So?' She gave him a playful, challenging smile. 'So?' she said again, softly, and it sounded like a dare.

'So I don't want to start something I have no intention of finishing amidst all these pots and pans,' Ben answered with just about the last shred of his self-control. 'Let's eat our dessert, or skip dessert even…'

'Now that sounds like a good idea.'

'We can go back to your room…'

Olivia just shook her head. 'I appreciate all the romance, Ben, I really do. But I want you here. Now.' And grabbing him by his shirt, she pulled him closer once more and kissed him.

The last of his self-control vanished. Olivia's hungry, open-mouthed kiss drop-kicked Ben's libido into the stratosphere, and he couldn't keep himself from kissing her back just as openly, just as hungrily.

He slid his hands under her dress and curved them round her bottom; her skin was warm and satiny, her underwear no more than a scrap of silk.

From reserves he never knew he had he managed to mutter, 'Not here...' but it must have sounded half-hearted at best because Olivia just pressed closer to him, one leg wound around his as she kissed away his words.

'Yes, here,' she said against his lips. 'Right here, right now. I don't want the fairy princess treatment. I want this to be real and raw and exciting.' She slid her hands up his chest and then pulled at his shirt, popping and scattering buttons. 'I have so much fake in my life, Ben. So much pretence.' Her voice went a little ragged, and she pulled again at his shirt. 'I want this to be real. I want it to be wild.' She slid his torn shirt from his shoulders and Ben groaned when she bent her head and bit his shoulder lightly. 'I want you to be wild. I know you can. I felt it from the moment I met you, and I want you now, feeling it for me.'

Ben's brain short-circuited as her words penetrated the red haze of his desire. She'd felt that energy, that anger, inside him—and she *liked* it? It turned her on? Some part of him instinctively rebelled at that thought, backed away from it, appalled—and another part, a far greater part, roared to life. Roared *yes*, that he wanted to lose the self-control he'd prized so highly; he wanted to be as real and raw and wild as Olivia wanted him to be. For once.

And that part won.

CHAPTER NINE

OLIVIA FELT THE moment when Ben's control snapped; it was like falling off the edge of the cliff. One moment he was holding her, his hands on her butt, his kiss full of hesitation and longing…

And the next he'd backed her up to one of the stainless-steel counters, spread her legs so his arousal was pressed up against her and kissed her with more hunger and passion than she'd ever felt from him before.

He pulled her dress up to her hips and then yanked it up higher, right to her waist, his face flushed and his pupils dilated as he slid his hand all the way up her leg, and then pressed his palm against the juncture of her thighs.

Olivia shuddered and Ben slid his hand underneath her underwear, fingers seeking her heat and finding it, oh, yes, finding it.

Their breathing was loud and ragged in the stillness of the kitchen, and the sound of the fragile fabric of her dress ripping as Ben pulled it over her head was like a screech. Olivia didn't care. She didn't care about anything but feeling more of this. She didn't want to hold anything back, and she didn't want Ben to either.

And he didn't. He kissed her hard on the mouth, and then moved lower, to the curve where her neck met her shoulder, and bit lightly, just as she had.

Sensation crashed over her and she squeezed her legs together, trapping his hand, her head falling onto his shoulder as she let out a shuddering breath.

'I think I'm going to…'

'Not yet, you aren't,' he answered, and withdrew his hand, much to Olivia's dismay, only to push her farther onto the counter so her body fell back and she lay there with her legs spread wide. Olivia had never felt so exposed, so *aware*, as she did sprawled on a stainless-steel counter with Ben standing between her legs. He got rid of her underwear in one quick tug, the flimsy material tearing, and then he pushed her thighs farther apart and bent his head to her.

Olivia arched upwards, letting out a cry of surprise and overwhelming pleasure as his mouth moved over her. He'd barely touched her and yet already she felt her climax crash over her; the intensity of it all, his mouth, his hands, the raw roughness of it, had simply been too much.

As soon as the aftershocks had died down to

mere tremors he pulled her upwards; she came bonelessly, her body sagging against his before he wrapped her legs around his waist and in one deep thrust buried himself inside her.

The feel of him inside her body was strange and wonderful, and while it didn't hurt, it took a moment for her to adjust and accept this sudden, intense invasion. Ben clamped his hands to her hips, guiding her to match her rhythm to his thrusts, and sparks of sensation seemed to shower through her whole body, lighting everything up inside her. She clutched his shoulders and brought her body even closer to his, found the pace and revelled in it.

He pressed her back against the counter, one hand braced against the steel as he moved inside her, harder and faster. The counter bit painfully into her back but Olivia didn't care. It only added to the intensity, that wildness she'd been craving. This was the most genuine thing she'd ever done, the most honest and real she'd ever been.

Then all those sparks burst into wondrous flame and her body tightened around his as they climaxed together.

For a few moments neither of them spoke, their bodies still wrapped around each other, the kitchen stretching out silently in every direction around them. Olivia could hear the thud of Ben's heart against hers.

Then slowly he eased away, disposing of the condom she hadn't even been aware of him putting on and reaching for his shirt. She let out a shuddering breath, her mind still spinning from everything she'd felt, physically and emotionally.

And true to form, because she didn't *do* intensity or emotion, no matter how much she craved both, she said the first inane thing that popped into her head.

'Sorry about your shirt.'

Ben glanced at the broken buttons and shrugged. 'It doesn't matter.' His voice was toneless, his face averted, and as Olivia watched him she became increasingly conscious that she was sitting on a cold, hard stainless-steel counter, wearing nothing but a bra. Her dress and underwear were on the floor, both torn beyond repair.

Ben was looping his belt through his trousers and so after a second Olivia slid off the counter and reached for her ruined dress.

All right, so this wasn't quite the kind of pillow talk she'd imagined. But she'd wanted wild and she'd got wild. Just the memory of all that raw, unrestrained passion made her feel like shivering. Her first sexual encounter had been *intense*. And amazing.

'So is the fondue ruined?' she asked, and to her humiliation her voice wobbled slightly. Okay, so maybe this part was a little hard. A little more exposing than she would have liked it to be.

Ben must have heard the wobble for he stopped getting dressed and turned to face her, taking her by the shoulders. 'Did I hurt you?' he asked, his voice a low growl, and Olivia blinked.

'What?' He'd asked her that before, she remembered. 'I'm aching in all sorts of interesting places, but no, I'm not *hurt.*'

He searched her face as if he suspected she was lying, but whatever he saw in her eyes—and Olivia had no idea what she looked like—must have satisfied him because he nodded once and released her.

'Good,' he said, and started dressing again. Olivia stared at him. She had no idea what was going on in his mind.

In his heart.

Whoa there, Olivia. Nothing is going on in his heart. Or yours. Don't confuse sex with love already.

'So.' She tucked her hair behind her ears, tried for a smile. 'What now?'

Ben looked up, his expression guarded, wary. Was he worried that she was going to start reading into things, asking for more?

'We could go back to my place,' she suggested. 'Or, really, your place. Since you were so keen on the bedroom idea.'

She raised her eyebrows, giving him what she hoped was a playful smile, praying she wasn't revealing just how much she wanted him to agree. How much she wanted the night not to end here, like this. Yes, she'd wanted wild, and she'd got wild. But she wanted something else now. She wanted closeness and companionship and comfort. She craved it as much as she had craved what had just happened between them.

'We could,' Ben agreed, and she couldn't tell a thing from his tone. 'But I have to clean up here first.'

'Let me help you,' Olivia suggested, and when Ben started to object she told him, 'I'd rather scrub pots and pans here with you than sit alone and wait for you in my suite.'

With a shrug of assent he started running hot water into the huge, industrial-size sink, and Olivia reached for the dish soap.

They spent a surprisingly pleasant half-hour washing dishes and chatting amicably about nothing too important or too intense; this was the kind of pillow talk she'd wanted, even if it happened to be over sponges and soap suds rather than while curled up on a king-size bed.

Ben was both funny and smart, and she enjoyed teasing and talking with him.

Enjoyed it too much, maybe.

It was easy, Olivia knew, to start building castles in the air after mind-blowing sex and interesting conversation. A dangerous combination, that.

Not, she told herself, that she was building castles or anything at all. She'd had a good time tonight, that was all. A *very* good time. But she wasn't looking for a relationship, never had been, and she didn't expect more from Ben Chatsfield than an incredible week.

She just needed to remind herself of that once in a while.

She wandered back out to the restaurant while Ben locked up and turned out the lights. The room was plunged into darkness, the city dark with only a few twinkling lights spread all around her.

Olivia stood in the middle, listening to Ben move around and trying to fight a sudden, intense wave of loneliness. There was absolutely no reason to feel lonely. No reason not to feel totally happy and satisfied. This was exactly what she'd wanted and no more. Intensity in bed and nowhere else. No emotion, no actual closeness...

She couldn't handle those things. She couldn't want them.

She heard his footsteps behind her and before she could turn around she felt his arms slip around her waist, drawing her against his chest. He bent his head and kissed the curve of her shoulder, the same place he'd bitten during their lovemaking.

Olivia closed her eyes, suppressing the sting of

tears. She didn't even know why she felt like crying. Maybe it had all been too much; she'd lived, by choice, in virtual emotional isolation for the past fourteen years, saving it all for the stage, and so perhaps tonight had been bound to wreck her.

Ben lifted his lips from her neck. 'Shall we go back?' he murmured, and wordlessly Olivia nodded.

They didn't speak as they headed out of the restaurant and into the elevator, and not when they walked down the corridor to Olivia's suite. She swiped the key card and stepped inside, Ben following her, neither of them speaking.

She headed towards the bedroom, because that was where she wanted to be, in Ben's arms again. Olivia stopped on the threshold, her breath coming out in a rush as she surveyed the transformed room. Candles flickered by the windows, casting shadows across the bed that was scattered with rose petals; their fragrance filled the air.

She turned to him, saw he was looking rather adorably self-conscious. 'You're actually a romantic, aren't you?'

'Only in certain situations.'

'Now I know why you wanted to go back to the bedroom,' Olivia said, and kissed him. His arms came around her and she fit herself to his body like she'd always been there; it was being away from him that had felt strange.

'This time it's going to be different,' Ben murmured.

'Not that different, I hope,' Olivia answered, and he laughed softly, no more than a breath of sound.

'We're going to take our time,' he told her, and then laid her gently down on the bed. The rose petals released their scent, the lovely fragrance seeming to wrap around her as Olivia lay on the bed and gazed up at Ben.

'I can see the benefits of a little romance,' she said, and he smiled, his hands going to his shirt.

'So can I. Definitely.'

'You don't actually have too many buttons to unbutton,' Olivia remarked as he started to undo his shirt. 'I kind of took care of that earlier.'

'A little excited, were you?'

'A little.'

He shrugged off his shirt, and she gloried in the sight of his bare chest, the taut, sleek muscle and sprinkling of dark chest hair veeing down to his trousers. He was such an unbelievably sexy man.

He stretched out next to her on the bed, wrapping his fingers around her ankle before sliding his hand slowly upwards, under her dress, across her belly and then finally to cup her breast. 'This dress,' he murmured, 'is a little in the way.'

'A little,' Olivia agreed again, and she wriggled around for Ben to unzip it. It was already torn just as his shirt was, but she was more than happy to consign the dress to the bin. Although on second thought, maybe she wouldn't. It certainly held some fond memories.

But as fond a memory as their time in the kitchen had been, Olivia knew this was already sweeter. Better. Ben's gentleness, as he cherished her body with his own, would be her undoing. He would unlock her heart.

And as he moved inside her, his gaze fastened to her own, a tenderness suffusing his face as he brought them both to climax, she thought that might actually be a wonderful thing.

Afterwards she lay amidst the rose petals, breathing in their fragrance as Ben lay next to her, his hand resting lightly on her belly. She felt, Olivia thought, almost perfectly happy. Too happy to worry or even think beyond this moment, beyond the sweet perfection of this night with Ben.

She rolled over so she could face him, simply because she wanted to look at him so much. She'd taken her turn touching and exploring him just as he had her, learning the taut muscles of his belly and the curve of his hip. Enjoying the feel of him, of knowing he was hers to explore and pleasure—at least for tonight.

Now she ran her fingertip along a wicked-looking scar that started under his arm and ran the length of his side, all the way to his hip.

'That looks like it was painful,' she said softly, and Ben didn't answer, just splayed his fingers along her belly. 'How did you get it?'

'Knife fight,' he said after a moment, and Olivia glanced up at his face, thinking for a second that he must be joking. She could tell from the hard set of his mouth and eyes that he wasn't.

'Goodness,' she said faintly. 'When were you in a knife fight?'

'When I first left home.' He rolled onto his back, stared up at the ceiling. 'I ended up in the south of France, in a dodgy section of Marseille. A couple of sailors jumped me.'

'That's horrible.' Ben just shrugged. 'Why did they jump you?' Olivia asked. 'And how did you get away?'

'They jumped me because I was an eighteen-year-old punk wandering around drunk in a bad neighbourhood. I got away because I fought back.' He spoke flatly, his face completely closed, and Olivia had the distinct feeling that he wasn't telling her something.

'I'm sorry,' she said quietly. 'That must have been terrible.'

'Not one of my better life experiences,' Ben agreed. 'But it wised me up at least.'

'No more wandering dark alleys?'

'Something like that.'

'Why did you leave home?' she asked after a

moment. She had a feeling these questions were semi-off-limits, although Ben hadn't said as much. They'd both agreed to a fling, but did that mean no heart-to-hearts? No actually getting to know each other? Because with her body still buzzing with satisfaction, she knew she wanted more than just the sex. She wanted to *know* this man.

'I didn't feel like I could stay,' Ben finally said. His tone was neither repressive nor particularly open; he was still staring at the ceiling.

'Because of your mother and her deception?'

'Yes.'

'Why not?'

'I know it doesn't seem to make sense,' he said after a moment. 'And sometimes I wonder if leaving was the wrong thing to do. But it felt like the only choice at the time.'

'I know how that feels,' Olivia said quietly. Ben turned to glance at her curiously, but didn't ask. And she was glad he didn't. She might have been asking some soul-baring questions, but she wasn't ready to answer her own, or explain how fourteen years after her mother's death the guilt at having disappointed her so terribly still haunted her. Drove her to make life a performance rather than something real.

Except you've been real with Ben.

Not that real though. Never that real. But she

was starting to want to be, which was a scary thought.

'Come on,' he said, nudging her bare shoulder. 'This evening's not over yet. And I want to try out that two-person shower.' He raised his eyebrows in invitation and Olivia laughed, grateful for the change in subject. And yes, she wanted to try that shower out too.

They spent a leisurely half-hour in the shower, soaping each other up and teasing each other unbearably, until Ben finally pulled her to him and sank inside her. Bliss.

Afterwards they towelled each other, everything strangely intimate and yet also weirdly normal. Amazing how quickly that had happened. Did that happen with everyone you had sex with, Olivia wondered, knowing she was being terribly naive by even wondering, or just with her and Ben? Did they have the beginnings of something special, or was she delusional?

'What is that?' Ben asked sharply, and Olivia blinked, jerked out of her little reverie. So much for warm fuzzies.

'What is what?' she asked, and Ben pointed to a rather large bruise, just coming up purple, on her hip.

'That.' His voice came out flat and hard, all the playful gentleness he'd been showing her evaporated along with the steam from the shower.

'Well.' Olivia examined it in some bemusement. She supposed she wouldn't be wearing her bikini any time soon. 'It's a bruise.'

'I know it's a bruise, Olivia,' Ben bit out. 'But how did you get it?'

'I assume from our activities in the kitchen,' she answered, trying to sound teasing. Why did he sound so…angry? 'That counter was made of steel, you know. It was kind of hard, and you were pushing me into it kind of ferociously.' She smiled, expecting him to smile back, to laugh about it, because bruise or not, it was kind of funny. Wasn't it?

Apparently Ben didn't think so. He glowered. 'I didn't—I didn't realise I was so rough.'

'You weren't that rough,' Olivia answered. Great, she was blushing. But this was kind of an awkward conversation. 'It's not like you were manhandling me. And anyway, I told you I wanted it wild.' She felt her cheeks heat even more. 'I like that about you, Ben. It feels…honest.'

'Honest?' He arched an eyebrow, coldly sceptical. 'Has anything about us been honest?'

Ouch. Now that hurt. More than it should, probably. 'I've thought so,' she said quietly, and felt the sting of tears behind her lids. Perfect. She was going to blush and cry. What an awesome way to cap off the evening. And just a few minutes ago she'd been covered in soap bubbles while Ben had kissed her senseless.

How had they got from there to here?

Ben was still staring at her bruise. Glaring at it, really. Olivia had no idea what had provoked this change in him, this bizarre anger. All she knew was she wanted what they'd had back. The gentleness and teasing and kisses.

'How about a drink?' she said, a bit desperately, because even though she was trying to hold on to it she sensed the evening and all of its promise slipping away from them.

'No. I need to get back.'

'Get back where?' She sounded almost as if she were whining. Cringe.

'I need to do some work.' Ben wrapped a towel around his waist and left the bathroom. Securing her own towel, Olivia followed him.

She would not beg, she told herself. No way. So he wanted to leave, fine. Had she really thought they'd cuddle all night? Besides, she needed her sleep, and she was pretty sure she'd find sleep difficult with Ben next to her. So this was good. All good.

'When will I see you again?' So much for playing it cool.

'I don't know.' Ben was dressing quickly, attempting to pull his shirt together despite the decided lack of buttons.

Olivia watched him, shivering in her towel, knowing it had all somehow gone wrong and not knowing what she could do to fix it. 'Ben...' she began, only to trail off helplessly.

He glanced at her, his expression dark and fathomless. She couldn't tell if there was any sympathy or understanding in that brooding gaze at all.

Then he reached out and cupped her cheek with his hand. Olivia closed her eyes, unable to keep herself from doing it, even as she willed tears not to fall.

'I'm sorry, Olivia,' he said, an ache in his voice, and it wasn't until he dropped his hand and had left the room that Olivia realised he hadn't actually said what he was sorry for.

And by that time he was gone.

CHAPTER TEN

SHE HAD A BRUISE. A bruise he'd given her. His stomach churned as Ben strode away from Olivia's suite. Logically, somewhere wrapped up in all the self-loathing and remorse, he knew he was overreacting. Knew that he hadn't meant to hurt Olivia, that she wasn't really that hurt to begin with, and it didn't have to be a big deal.

But still, a bruise. A bruise he had caused without even being aware of it because he'd given in to the *wildness* she'd sensed in him. The same wildness that had once left a man unconscious and bleeding on a deserted street, as close to death as any man ever could be.

And as for tonight…memories came trickling back, icy and unwelcoming. Pushing Olivia back against the counter. Thrusting inside her without even remembering that this was her first time. Feeling totally out of control, overwhelmed by emotion, *savage*.

God help him, what had he been thinking?

Doing? No wonder Olivia had seemed a little uncertain afterwards. Ben was amazed she hadn't backed away, fear on her face. But maybe she hadn't realised just how out of control he'd been. How consumed.

Scrubbing his face with his hands, Ben headed upstairs for the pool. He needed to swim some laps.

A couple of hours later he lay in bed and stared up at the ceiling of his bedroom, his head pillowed on one arm, his mind blazing with images of Olivia, memories he wanted to cherish despite his own despicable actions.

He pictured her smiling saucily at him as she licked chocolate off a strawberry. Kissing him in the kitchen. Wrapping her legs around his waist as she drew him deeper inside her. Lying with her on the huge bed, surrounded by rose petals, feeling happier than he had in a long, long time. Telling her things about himself, because he'd actually wanted to. Because it seemed like she understood.

And then seeing that bruise.

One little bruise, but it showed him who he really was. How he hadn't changed. He still had the anger inside him, despite fourteen years of rigid control. Coming back here, being with a woman who actually affected him…it brought it all back.

The anger he'd felt when his father had told him

Spencer was a bastard, his childhood a lie. The rage he'd felt when six sailors had knocked him down and he'd just kept punching and punching, even after they'd begged him to stop. The sudden, surprising fury that had choked him when Spencer had walked into his restaurant, as easy as you please, after fourteen years of silence. So much anger. He was so damn tired of feeling it. He'd tried, over the years, to let it go. He'd pushed the feelings far down deep inside and for a while it had seemed he'd managed to forget them completely. Coming back here had shown him he hadn't.

And it had also shown him he didn't have the strength or space in his life for a relationship, not even a fling. He didn't trust himself not to hurt her. Not to lose control again, and worse.

From now on it was pretend only for the public, nothing more. Even if everything in him still ached for Olivia.

'So what exactly is going on with you and Ben Chatsfield?'

'Huh?' Olivia looked up from the magazine she'd been flicking through and tossed it aside with a sigh. 'Why are you even asking that question, Melissa?' she asked her agent. 'You know what's going on. Nothing.' She smiled, her eyebrows raised. 'But I'm glad the publicity is working.'

'I'm not sure it is,' Melissa answered with a frown.

'What do you mean?' Olivia rose from her seat and paced the room restlessly; they were cooling their heels in Melissa's suite while waiting for a photo call for *Blue Skies Forever*. 'Actually, I'm not sure I want to know. I can't handle any more stress right now.' Melissa just watched her, frowning, and Olivia collapsed onto a sofa with a defeated sigh. 'Okay, fine, tell me. What's not working?'

'It's just a bit up and down, isn't it?' Melissa said carefully. 'First there was the photo of Ben practically pushing you away from him after that kiss—and what a kiss! And then the next night you're wrapped around each other on the dance floor, and you leave a high-profile party very early.'

Olivia could feel her face starting to heat but still managed to stare her agent down. 'So?'

'And then the next night word gets out that Ben has closed The Chatsfield's restaurant, which put several noses out of joint and made all the tabloids speculate.'

Olivia swallowed. 'I still don't see what the problem is. We're supposedly in a relationship. Of course the media is going to take note. Ben Chatsfield is a celebrity chef after all.'

'And you're an up-and-coming actress,' Melissa added with a smile. 'But it's still a bit much, Olivia. It isn't the kind of publicity the producers of this film want.'

Olivia shifted in her seat, fury and despair warring within her. After everything, she still might not get this role, thanks to her big mouth and Ben Chatsfield? 'What kind of publicity do they want then?' she asked, aware she sounded sulky.

'They want to see you acting like a mature, confident woman in a committed relationship. Not blowing hot and cold and seeming…unstable.'

'Unstable,' Olivia repeated in disbelief. 'Look, I wasn't the one who pushed anyone away.'

'You know what I mean. Could you talk to Ben? Maybe appear at a party or premiere, something low-key, holding hands, looking calm and together?'

Calm and together. Right. Because that's exactly what they were.

Not.

'Sure,' she said wearily. 'I'll talk to him.' Even though he'd been avoiding her for the past forty-eight hours, since he'd stormed out of her suite after their shower. She still didn't understand what that was about, and the fact that Ben was choosing to ignore her hurt more—a lot more—than she knew it should. The thought of asking him for a favour now made everything in her curl up and cringe.

But if she wanted to secure this film role, it appeared she had no choice.

With the photo call finished and Olivia's feet aching from the supposedly sensible taupe heels she'd worn, she went in search of Ben. His PA informed her that he was out of the office, and refused to give any more information than that.

'Do you know when he'll be back?' Olivia asked the woman, realising that as Ben's girl-friend she should have his cell number, not to mention know where he was.

'I have no idea,' the woman answered frostily, and Olivia eyed her with speculation. Looked like there might be a little crush on the boss going on. She'd have to watch her back.

'Thank you,' she murmured, and not knowing what else to do, she headed outside. She couldn't stand moping about her hotel suite any longer.

February in Berlin was, as she'd discovered every time she'd stepped out of The Chatsfield, cold. It wasn't raining now, but the sky was heavy and grey and low and Olivia hunched into her down parka as she walked down Stulerstrasse, towards the Tiergarten.

Once inside the huge park she wandered down the tree-lined boulevards, the branches now stark and bare. In a small cluster of tables and bunches, a few hardy Berliners sat eating, Olivia saw from the vendor's cart nearby, crispy pork knuckles. She'd pass.

At another cart she bought an espresso and sipped it as she walked along, wishing she didn't feel quite so miserable. The night before last had been the most amazing of her life. Just remembering the way Ben had looked at her, with such tenderness and sincerity, and all the trouble he'd gone to—the restaurant and the rose petals and the rest of it…

All of it brought a lump of longing to Olivia's throat. She might not have agreed to lose her virginity to Ben if she'd known she'd feel this bad afterwards. But how could she have known that Ben would have hightailed out of her suite the way he had, and then do his best to pretend she didn't exist?

So their time together had been a little shorter than she'd expected. The end result had always been going to be the same. It had to be.

Sighing, she rose from the bench and headed back to the hotel. She found Ben's PA, saw how the woman turned sour as soon as she caught sight of Olivia and suppressed a sigh.

'Is Ben in?'

'Mr Chatsfield,' the woman informed her loftily, 'is busy…'

'But is he in his office?'

The woman hesitated, and without waiting for

a reply, Olivia pushed past her and opened the door to Ben's office.

And there he was, looking tired and hassled and utterly delicious. His hair, as usual, was sexily rumpled. His suit was creased, stubble glinting on his jaw. He looked good enough to eat. Olivia opened her mouth to say something and found she couldn't say anything at all. A huge lump had formed in her throat, and there was no getting past that sucker.

Ben looked up and his gaze narrowed on her. He didn't say hello, didn't even smile. And suddenly Olivia found she could speak past that lump.

'Look, I need a favour.'

'A favour? Why?'

Not *Anything for you, Olivia*, or *How are you, Olivia, since I took your maidenhead?* Not that she'd been fantasising or anything.

'Because of that stunt you pulled the other night, pushing me away,' Olivia snapped. Yes, why didn't they fight? It was better than her bursting into tears and asking him why he'd pushed her away—not in front of the cameras but when they were alone. When she'd given him her body and maybe even her heart.

No, Olivia. You weren't that stupid.

Except she had a horrible feeling she might have been.

'I didn't pull a stunt,' Ben said coolly. 'And I already apologised for reacting that way, and explained why I did.'

'Well, as it happens, we now have to do some damage control,' Olivia shot back. She still sounded snippy.

Ben glowered, as if he couldn't imagine anything worse than spending yet another evening with her. *And forty-eight hours ago you were showering me with rose petals as you kissed me everywhere...*

Olivia blinked hard.

'What do we have to do?' he asked.

'If it's not too much trouble,' she told him, piling on the sarcasm, 'then you can accompany me to a charity benefit tonight. We can stay low-key, no posing for the cameras. Just show up, stay a few hours and act civil and then leave.'

'Fine.' He turned back to his computer, effectively dismissing her.

Olivia stood there for a bit, staring, stunned. 'Fine,' she finally repeated numbly, and walked out.

Ben pushed hard away from his desk and spun in his chair. *That went well.*

He'd seen the hurt in Olivia's eyes and he'd chosen to ignore it. Maybe that made him an emotional coward, but it seemed like the better option than explaining to her that he wasn't interested in anything with her, not even a fling, because he didn't trust himself.

Easier for you, you bastard. He knew with a gut-wrenching certainty that it hadn't been easy for Olivia, not knowing why he was pulling away, and guilt ate away any resolve he'd been hanging on to.

But what was the alternative? Tell her the truth? That possibility made everything in him shrink in shame and horror. He'd rather she thought he was a bastard for ignoring her than know the truth of what he really was—and what he was capable of.

'Mr Chatsfield?'

His PA, Rebecca, stood in the doorway, and Ben forced a smile.

'Yes, Rebecca?'

'Is...is everything okay? It just seemed like that Harrington woman was kind of...difficult.'

'I handled it, it's fine.' Too late Ben realised he shouldn't have talked that way about his alleged girlfriend. Shaking his head, he rose from the desk. 'We were just discussing our plans tonight,' he added, and Rebecca looked incredulous.

Who could blame her, Ben thought as he headed out of his office. He wasn't exactly doing a spectacular job as a boyfriend, real or pretend.

Olivia gazed at her reflection and frowned. The pale gold sheath dress was the last fancy outfit in her wardrobe; the extra birthday party with Ben had depleted her fashion resources. She'd thrown this dress in as an emergency measure, and now she wondered if it really worked. Its clean, simple lines might be a little on the dull side, but the shimmery material hopefully made up for that. Her silver pendant didn't really go with the gold, but she hadn't taken that necklace off in fourteen years and she wasn't going to tonight.

She touched the lopsided heart with its overlapping edges and thought of her mother's words as she'd given it to her.

Because my love for you will go on and on, Olivia, just like this heart. It never stops. It will never end.

She closed her eyes, guilt and grief twisting inside her. She tried not to think about her mom too much, or how much she'd let her down. It hurt even to think about the necklace. But she'd still keep it on. Always.

A knock sounded at the door, a short rat-a-tat-tat that had Olivia opening her eyes and grimacing at her reflection. Ben had arrived.

She opened the door, tried to keep her expression neutral as she took in his black trousers and white dress shirt, an outfit that should be boring and ordinary but of course looked amazing on Ben. It simply wasn't fair for him to be so abominably attractive.

He nodded his greeting. 'Are you ready?'

No compliments about how fantastic she looked or amazing she was tonight, Olivia noted sourly. Had he ever meant any of it? Maybe he'd just been trying to get her into bed.

Of course he was, you idiot.

He'd made no bones about that and yet it still hurt that he'd dropped her like a hot potato the moment he'd got what he'd wanted.

'Yes, I'm ready.' She reached for her matching bag and wrap and headed out into the corridor, not even looking at Ben as he fell into step beside her. Still she could feel the tension between them, and not the exciting, sexual kind. It tautened the air as they stepped into the lift, both of them staring ahead, Ben with his arms folded, looking as if he'd rather be just about anywhere else.

'You're going to have to up your game if you want the public to believe we're actually dating,' Olivia snapped in the seconds before the doors opened onto the lobby. 'You look one step up from being tortured.'

He looked as if he were about to fire off a retort in kind when he shut his mouth with a snap and looked away. 'I'm sorry,' he said, and Olivia had no idea—again—what he was sorry for. But this time she was going to ask.

'What are you sorry for?' she asked as they stepped out of the lift and she stretched her mouth into a smile, even let out a little, tinkling laugh as if she were having the time of her life with the man in her life.

'Olivia…'

'Are you sorry, for example, for running away from me as fast as you could after having got what you wanted?'

'I did not run away…' Ben interjected, his jaw like granite.

'Or,' Olivia continued, still smiling, 'for ignoring me for the next forty-eight hours?'

'I was busy with something called a job…'

'Or maybe it's the charming way you've behaved since I saw you in your office this afternoon? As if you couldn't so much as bear the sight of me?'

'That's not true.'

'Really?' They stepped outside the hotel, the cold air like a slap in the face. 'You could have fooled me,' she said, and raised her arm to hail a cab.

Satisfyingly, one pulled to the kerb with a screech and Olivia slid inside. Ben followed, his leg nudging hers before he moved away, his hands resting on his thighs.

'I'm sorry,' he said after a moment when Olivia had given the address of the benefit and they'd moved off into the traffic streaming down Stulerstrasse, 'for leaving the way I did, without explaining. And for not coming to talk to you since then. And for acting as if I didn't want to see you when you came and found me.' He turned to her then with a bleak smile that shouldn't have made Olivia ache but did anyway. A lot. 'So you see,' he said, his voice low and rough, 'I'm sorry for all the things you said. And more.'

'More?' Olivia whispered when she'd finally found her voice. 'What more is there, Ben?'

He turned to the window and she thought he wouldn't answer her. Then he said, his voice an ache, 'For not being able to be the man you want and need me to be.'

'And what kind of man is that?' Olivia asked. Her throat was so tight it hurt to get the words out.

'I can't...' He let out a low breath. 'I can't explain.'

'Can't or won't?'

'Both.' He turned to her with such sadness and even agony in his eyes that Olivia nearly gasped aloud. 'I don't want you to hate me, Olivia. I don't want you to look at me with derision or worse. So can we just call time on what we had, and remember how good it was?'

She stared at him, torn between hurt, confusion and a deep empathy even though she had no idea why he thought she might hate him. 'We were only talking about a fling, Ben,' she finally said. 'A week or two. What happened to make you change your mind about that?'

He looked out the window again. 'I just realised it was a mistake.'

'It? You mean me. *I* was a mistake.'

'Our affair.'

'Our one-night stand,' she corrected, the words bitten off and spat out.

'Fine. Yes.'

Olivia slumped against the seat, suddenly exhausted by their wrangling. And what purpose did it even serve? Whatever they had, whatever either one of them called it, it was over. The end. And she should let it go and get on with her life.

The cab pulled up to the front of the impressive Neues Museum, where the benefit was being held. A line of limos and cabs snaked down the drive, while women in evening gowns and cocktail dresses and men in a wide array of evening dress mounted the front steps to the museum.

With a sigh Olivia opened the door of the cab. 'Let's get this over with,' she said.

She joined the throng of celebrity guests, stretching her lips into a smile that felt like her worst performance ever as the paparazzi called out and the flashbulbs popped. Ben walked by her side, and to her surprise, as a reporter aimed a camera at them, he reached for her hand, threading his fingers through hers.

A lump rose in Olivia's throat. It had been only forty-eight hours, and she knew he was only holding her hand for the cameras, but she'd *missed* him. She'd missed this closeness.

They passed the photographers and Ben slipped his hand from hers.

The party was, as Olivia had known it would be, nearly intolerable. After an hour enduring several stilted conversations as they circulated the grand foyer of the museum, glasses of champagne in hand, she was ready to go. Ben had smiled and chatted with apparent ease, fooling, Olivia suspected, everyone but her.

She felt his tension, even his anger. She could almost hear it, like a thrumming in the air, or as if a live wire connecting them shivered and pulsed.

Silly, fanciful thoughts, and yet she could not deny the sense of connection she felt with Ben, even when he was doing his best to be distant. His desolate words from the cab echoed through her. *I don't want you to hate me, Olivia. I don't want you to look at me with derision or worse.*

Why on earth would he say or even think such a thing? What secret was he hiding that he believed if she knew would make her turn away from him?

Or was she jumping to conclusions? Yet what else could he have meant?

She knew about secrets. She knew about guilt.

The thought of admitting her own made her wince and cringe. Was Ben the same? Did they have that in common too? If she admitted her own, would that help Ben to open up?

The question horrified her, but it also wouldn't leave her alone. She didn't want to be that honest. That intimate.

Then what are you playing at here, Olivia? Call time like Ben said or go all in. It's one or the other.

Suddenly she couldn't stand being at this party for another minute, being fake with everyone, especially Ben. Abruptly she turned to him.

'Let's go.'

He stared at her, unsmiling. 'We've only been here an hour.'

'I'm done,' she said flatly. 'Done with pretending. I want to go.'

Surprise flickered across his features and slowly he nodded. 'Okay,' he said, and took her arm before heading towards the doors.

Outside the museum the paparazzi sprang into action as soon as they exited the doors. The questions came thick and fast, as there was no one else around to distract the voracious reporters.

'Olivia, is there trouble between you and Ben? Is that why you're leaving early?'

'Why did he push you away outside the premiere of your film? Not happy with your *perfor-*

mance?' Olivia blinked, startled by the sneering innuendo of the male reporter who pushed his camera close to her face. 'Maybe it was your performance outside of the film that disappointed him?' the man continued with an obvious leer.

Shock iced through Olivia as the blood drained from her face. 'No comment,' she whispered, but the reporter had sensed he'd struck a nerve and so he pushed on.

'There must be some reason Ben is throwing you over...'

'Back off,' Ben said, and Olivia stilled at the quiet, deadly venom in his voice. The reporter was oblivious.

'Were you hoping dating Ben Chatsfield would save the family business—or help your struggling career?'

'No...' Olivia's voice cut off as if someone had grabbed her by the throat. But no one had; it was the reporter who was being grabbed, and Olivia watched in disbelief as Ben yanked the man to his tiptoes by grabbing the front of his shirt.

'Back. Off.' He stared at the man, his knuckles white as he held him by the shirt, and the man stared at him goggle-eyed as cameras snapped.

'Ben,' Olivia said quietly.

Slowly she saw awareness dawn in Ben's face. He released the man's shirt and took a step back. Took a deep breath and let it out slowly. He nodded once, although whether in apology or acknowledgement Olivia didn't know. Then he took her by the hand and led her to the sanctuary of a waiting cab.

CHAPTER ELEVEN

HE'D THREATENED A MAN.

Ben had to keep his body from shaking as he slid into the cab, angled his face away from Olivia. He had no idea what she was thinking, how horrified she must be. Adrenalin raced through him and he raked his hands through his hair before doubling over as nausea suddenly swamped him.

'Are you all right?' she asked quietly.

He clamped his jaw tight as an icy sweat broke over his body. Then he straightened, keeping his face turned away from her. 'I'm fine.'

Except he wasn't fine, not remotely. In fourteen years he'd never come so close to doing another person bodily harm. He drew a shuddering breath as the nausea crashed over him once more.

'Pull the car over,' he snapped to the driver, and alarmed, the man screeched to the kerb.

Ben threw the door open, bent over and was sick in the gutter.

Olivia sat there, frozen in shock, as he shut the

door, then eased back against the seat and closed his eyes.

'Drive,' he said, and with an alarmed look for the pair of them, the cabbie pulled back into the traffic.

Olivia stared at him, his eyes still closed, his face pale, and was torn between comforting him and demanding answers.

In the end she said nothing, figuring they both needed a moment to compose themselves, and then the cab was pulling up in front of The Chatsfield and a bellhop was opening the door. She slid out of the taxi and Ben followed, striding ahead of her into the hotel.

He seemed set to keep walking and just leave her there with nothing but a nod goodbye, but Olivia wasn't having it.

'Ben,' she said quietly, and he stilled. Said nothing. 'We need to talk.' She waited, her heart pounding, conscious of the people all around them, the curious looks. She did not want to have a showdown with Ben in the lobby of The Chatsfield, but she wasn't going to let him walk away from her either. Not after everything that had happened tonight. Everything that she didn't understand, but knew she wanted to.

'I know,' Ben said, and with an air of resignation he turned towards the bank of elevators.

Neither of them spoke again until they were in the privacy of Olivia's suite. She dropped her clutch and wrap on the hall table and went to the living area.

'I don't know about you, but I'm ready to raid the minibar.' She went to the bar in the corner and pulled out a small bottle of cognac, twisted off the cap and downed half of it in one long, burning swallow.

She hissed as the alcohol blazed through her, and then turned to face Ben. He stood with his hands in his pockets, his face expressionless yet with a weary resignation to the hunch of his shoulders. Silently she handed him the bottle.

With the barest quirk of a smile he took it and had a long swallow.

'Tell me what's going on,' she said.

He lifted his shoulders in a shrug, his face still blank as he put the little bottle of cognac on top of the bar. 'You saw what went on.'

'I saw you nearly hit a reporter and then get a case of the shakes when you got in the cab…'

'I wasn't shaking,' Ben cut her off quietly.

'Are you going to pretend you weren't sick in the street either?' His expression closed right up then and he looked away. *'Ben.'* She took a step towards him, arms outstretched. 'Ben, you've said and done things I don't understand tonight and I *need* to understand them, for my own peace of mind, and maybe for yours. Please don't shut me out. I have no idea what's going on or what is… *tormenting* you, but I want to know.' She took a deep breath, her own emotions scraped raw, so close to the surface. 'I want to help.'

'You can't help.' He spoke flatly, with finality, and Olivia shook her head slowly.

'Maybe you should let me be the judge of that.'

Ben stared at her; his hazel eyes seemed to burn right through her, his jaw so tight she could see the muscles bunched. 'You want to know?' he finally said, and it wasn't a question. 'Fine. You can know. You deserve that much.' He took a breath, let it out slowly. 'I nearly killed a man once.'

She blinked, her mind trying to process that statement, which was so not what she'd been expecting. Although she hadn't known what to expect, but…it hadn't been that.

'Okay,' she finally said, and Ben raised his eyebrows, his mouth twisting unpleasantly.

'Okay? You think it's okay that I nearly beat a man to death and left him for dead in the street?'

She blinked again, scrambling now for something to say, to think. 'No, of course it's not okay. But I feel like you're trying to shock me, maybe make me feel disgusted by you, as if that's something you'd actually want.' She didn't know where the words came from exactly, but she knew they were true. She lifted her chin and tried to stare him down. 'And I'm not going to do that, Ben. I won't make it that easy for you.'

'Nothing about this is easy.'

'So tell me more. Who was this man?'

'One of the sailors who jumped me in Marseille.'

'And you defended yourself.'

'Don't try to justify it, Olivia.'

'I'm not…'

'Yes, you are. You want to, because you don't want to believe what kind of man I am.'

'And what kind of man are you, Ben?' Olivia challenged. 'A monster?' He didn't answer. 'This is why you thought I would hate you,' she said slowly. 'Why you thought I would be disgusted by you. Why you got so angry when you saw that bruise.'

He shook his head impatiently, stalking away from her. 'You don't understand.'

'Then tell me.'

He paced the room, one hand driven though his hair, his head bowed. Olivia watched and waited. Finally he spoke. 'I've been angry, more or less, for fourteen years.'

'Angry,' Olivia repeated. *That wildness.*

That wildness she'd felt inside him, that energy that excited her…that was *anger*?

'What are you angry about?' she asked as Ben continued to pace.

'It doesn't matter. The point is, I can't control

it. I let it out when those sailors jumped me and one of them ended up almost dead.'

'Yeah, I got that part. But I think it does matter. How can you deal with your anger, Ben, if you're not willing to acknowledge…'

'I don't need psychotherapy, Olivia,' he snapped. 'I just need to control my emotions, and I can't. That's why I've pulled away from you. Why I haven't been in a serious relationship, ever. Because I don't trust myself.'

'Do you think you'll hurt me?' she asked slowly, and Ben turned to face her, his face contorted with what looked and felt like agony.

'I don't want to hurt anyone. But I gave you that bruise…'

'A bruise, Ben, not a broken nose!' She shook her head. 'I was the one who wanted it wild and even rough.' And just saying that could still make her blush with the memory of it. 'You would have taken my virginity on a bed of rose petals. Literally.'

He just shook his head. 'You didn't know…'

'No, I didn't,' she cut him off quietly as she took a step towards him. 'I didn't know you had all this anger inside you, but I sensed something good inside you, Ben. The flip side of that anger, maybe. A passion that was honest and real and exciting to me.' She took a deep breath. 'I see it in the way you cook. In your drive to succeed.

In how you kissed me. I like your emotion, Ben. Your wildness.'

'Only because you didn't know the truth of it.'

'That you beat up a sailor who jumped you fourteen years ago? No, I didn't know that, but it doesn't…'

'Maybe you should read the hospital report before you excuse everything away,' Ben told her in a hard voice. 'A broken nose, a shattered cheekbone and a dislocated jaw. And I just walked away.'

'With a knife wound,' she reminded him and he just shrugged 'How did you find the hospital report?'

'I looked for it later. I wanted—I wanted to make sure I hadn't killed him.'

She felt tears crowd her eyes and she blinked them back. 'So how long are you going to torture yourself for one mistake, big as it might have been?' she asked in a shaky voice. 'One episode doesn't define you, Ben.'

'No?' he challenged quietly. 'What if that one episode reveals you? Shows what you're really like?'

She just blinked then, because she had no answer for that one. She'd felt the same about herself. Choosing to let her mother down in her darkest hour had defined her character and all the choices she'd made since it had happened…

fourteen years ago. Just like Ben she'd been living with the guilt of a single, regrettable action.

He nodded, his mouth curving in a grim smile. 'You don't have an answer for that one, do you?'

'No,' she said slowly, 'but not because of you. Because of me.'

'What do you mean?'

She knew then that she couldn't demand honesty from Ben and keep back her own secrets. Her own shame. And maybe hearing about her struggles would help Ben with his.

'Well,' she said after a moment, her voice wobbling all over the place, 'I made a big mistake just like you did, once upon a time.'

He frowned, his gaze moving over her face, searching for answers. 'What do you mean?'

'I let my mom down. In the biggest way possible.'

His expression softened then, and with a weak laugh that was far too close to a sob Olivia sank onto the sofa. She'd never told anyone any of this, ever.

'What happened, Olivia?' Ben asked quietly.

'When she got sick, I mean really sick…' She stopped, took a breath that tore at her lungs. 'Let me go back a bit,' she said after a few seconds' pause when she struggled to maintain her composure. She knew she needed to tell Ben this, and maybe he needed to hear it. But it was hard. 'I was my mother's favourite. I'm not saying that to be mean or arrogant or something…'

'I believe you,' Ben interjected quietly, and she fell silent, managed a very shaky smile.

'We just had a bond. We did so much together. We were similar, kind of shy to begin with but with a flair for the dramatic. She also encouraged my acting, which is why…' She stopped then, because her chest hurt and her throat was going tight. After a moment she resumed. 'We laughed a lot together, over the silliest stuff. And then she got sick when I was twelve. It was only a couple of months—she went downhill pretty quickly. But I…' Her throat closed up and she drew in a revealingly clogged breath.

'Olivia,' Ben said quietly, and he came to sit beside her, reached for her hand. Olivia clung to it as if it were a life preserver in this sudden sea of emotion she was drowning in.

'I bailed,' she said simply. 'On her. On everything. The sicker she became, the less I was around. She used to ask me to come sit next to her and tell her about my day, simple stuff, and I'd find any excuse not to.' Olivia felt two tears slip down her cheeks and she dashed them away with her free hand. 'Any excuse not to spend time with her. And I could see how it hurt her, and still I did it.' She shook her head, more tears slipping down her face as a sob rose in her chest, a howl of guilt and grief and regret.

Ben didn't say anything, and Olivia thought she must have shocked him. Disgusted him with her selfish, terrible behaviour. Her choice *had* revealed her. It hadn't been like his, one moment of uncontrollable anger, deeply regretted. It had been a thousand little wounds, given deliberately, over a course of months. Of course it revealed her.

The pressure built in her chest and she knew she wouldn't be able to keep it in. Like Ben, she'd stuffed her emotions down for so long. Tried to pretend they didn't exist. And the intensity and passion they'd felt for each other had brought everything out to the glaring light. There was no hiding now. No pretending to be someone else.

And she still didn't like who she was. Hated Ben knowing. She pushed away from him, averting her face.

Gently Ben reached out and cupped her cheek, turning her to face him. 'Olivia, you were twelve.'

'Oh, so that's my excuse?' she retorted, drawing back.

Ben gave her a quiet, sad smile. 'And mine was self-defence, remember?'

'It's different, Ben.'

'How is it different?'

She shook her head. 'Because—because it's *me*.'

Ben nodded, understanding gleaming in his

eyes. 'Okay, so one set of rules for you, one set for everyone else?'

'We're talking about my mother, the person I loved best. And I failed her. Utterly.' She felt the pressure inside her building again, and her words came faster, harder. 'Do you know what my last conversation with her was?' she demanded, and with sorrowful eyes Ben shook his head.

'No.'

'She asked me to come in and sit on her bed, and I wouldn't. I stayed by the door, looking like I was itching to get away, which I was.' Olivia drew in a choking breath. 'And she said, "Livvy, I love you so much. You know that, don't you?"' The silence of that unanswered question hung in the air between them, echoed terribly inside Olivia. 'Do you know what I said?' she whispered, and wordlessly Ben drew her back into his arms. 'Nothing,' she said dully, and closed her eyes. 'I didn't answer at all. I didn't tell her I knew, or that I loved her back. I just sloped off to my room and when I woke up the next morning she was dead.'

Ben's arms tightened around her as she sobbed into his shoulder, holding nothing back. She hadn't cried like this, hadn't let herself cry like this, since her mother had died. Some part of her had insisted she didn't deserve to cry, didn't have the right to grief, not when she'd been so horribly selfish. But she knew she needed to cry, to let it all out. Finally.

Eventually the tears subsided and Olivia remained there, her cheek still resting against Ben's shoulder. She felt as exhausted as if she'd just run a marathon. And she supposed she had, in a way. An emotional marathon.

After a long moment Ben eased back and, brushing the damp strands of hair away from her face, looked down at her. 'I'm glad you told me,' he said quietly. 'And I'm going to tell you the same kind of thing you told me. What you did when you were twelve, when you were scared and sad and under pressure, doesn't define *or* reveal you.'

'She was my mother, my mom…'

'And why do you think you avoided her?' Ben asked.

'Because I hated seeing her like that. Shrivelled and wasting away. It scared me so much, because I knew it meant she would leave me.' The words bubbled up from a hidden place deep inside her. 'So I suppose I tried to pretend it wasn't happening, even though I knew it hurt her.'

'And don't you think that's at least a little understandable? If it was someone else, some other twelve-year-old girl, wouldn't you give her a break?'

'Maybe,' Olivia admitted, even though she knew she never would have judged someone else in the same position. 'But it's different because it's me. And my mother. Because I can still see the look on her face when she told me she loved me, and I didn't say anything back.' Her throat thickened again. 'I don't get a redo on that one, Ben. I can never change that or take it back. That's how my mother will have remembered me. Glaring at her while she was telling me she loved me.'

Ben was quiet for a moment. 'I'm guessing your mother was mature enough to realise that just because you hadn't said the words, didn't mean you didn't feel them. She knew you loved her, Olivia.'

'But I still can't take it back,' Olivia whispered.

'But you can forgive yourself,' Ben answered steadily. 'You can cherish the good memories you had with your mother and move on. Do you think she'd want you to hold back from life, from people, because of what you did? Because that's what you've done, isn't it? That's why you haven't had any serious relationships, why you were still a virgin.'

'I didn't trust myself not to let someone down,' Olivia whispered. 'I still don't. And I didn't... I didn't feel I deserved...' Her voice broke and he took her in his arms once more.

'Oh, Olivia. You're one of the strongest, funniest, kindest people I know. You deserve so much love and happiness, and I know, absolutely, that your mother would want it for you.'

Olivia closed her eyes, wanting to believe him, beginning to believe it even as she acknowledged the tone Ben had used. The tone of someone who was wishing you well, someone who wouldn't be the person who gave you that love and happiness.

He thought she deserved love and happiness… but he still didn't think he did.

She took a deep breath. 'And what about you, Ben? You've absolved me, but I know absolutely that one mistake, one moment, doesn't define a person or his character. That's shown through a lifetime of moments, of decisions and choices. And it seems like you've chosen to control your anger. To live responsibly.'

Ben stiffened, drawing away from her. 'Can you really say that, when I nearly punched a man tonight?'

'He was an ass,' Olivia answered. 'And the important thing is, you *didn't* punch him. You let go of him. You know what that's called? Self-control.'

Ben just shook his head. 'You don't know…'

'Then tell me. What are you angry about, Ben? What's driving you still?' He shook his head again. 'You need to forgive yourself for being angry,' Olivia insisted. 'Whatever its source. And for beating up that guy.'

'And how do you go about doing that?' Ben asked after a moment. 'How do you just let a feeling go? Because God knows if I could, I would.'

'I don't know,' Olivia admitted honestly. 'Maybe it's a process.'

Ben closed his eyes. 'I'm so tired of it all. Tired of being angry.'

'If I could help you to let go of it, I would.' Olivia slipped from the sofa to kneel in front of him. His head was lowered and she slid her hands through his hair, drawing his head up so he was facing her. Then she kissed him.

There was no wildness now. There was only gentleness and peace, a kiss of absolution. Ben brought his hands up to her shoulders, steadied hers as he kissed her back. And such a sweet, sweet kiss it was.

The gentleness turned to urgency, but still it wasn't rough or wild. It was immediate and necessary and good, right there in the living room, as Ben peeled the dress from her body and she undid the buttons of his shirt. Carefully. Tenderly. Every movement telling him this was okay.

And it was more than okay; it was wonderful, overwhelmingly so, to have him touching her again. Loving her again. He lay her down on the rug right there in the living room and covered her body with his own, his face buried in her neck as Olivia wrapped herself around him and brought him into her body. Into her very self.

Afterwards they lay clinging together, their bodies completely entwined, their hearts thudding against each other. Slowly Ben eased off, gazed down at her. Gently he brushed a tendril of hair away from her cheek.

'Did I…?'

'Hurt me?' she finished. 'No, of course not.'

He sighed and lightly rested his forehead against hers. 'Thank you,' he whispered.

Gazing up at him, at the tenderness in his eyes, Olivia felt her heart lurch. Her world shift. She loved this man. This fascinating, complex, tender, angry man.

And as he rolled off her, she had no idea if he felt anything back, or if what they'd just shared had been a moment of intensity brought on by all they'd shared, and nothing more.

CHAPTER TWELVE

BEN WOKE UP to pale, winter sunlight streaming in through the floor-to-ceiling windows of Olivia's bedroom. Memories of the night before sifted through his mind, the heart-wrenching conversation, the mind-blowing sex. And afterwards, the sweet companionship. He'd made them both pasta and they'd chatted and laughed, all of it amazingly easy after what had gone before. He'd asked if he could stay the night, and the smile that had bloomed across her face had been a balm to his soul.

He'd slept with her wrapped around him, their legs tangled together, her arm across his waist. He couldn't remember the last time he'd slept so well.

He glanced down at her now, her hair spread across the white pillowcase, her lashes feathering her cheeks, her lips slightly pursed. She looked beautiful, of course, but he also saw a touching vulnerability in the roundness of her cheek, the sweep of her lashes. He ran his thumb gently down her cheek, thinking of all she'd shared, all the heartache she'd endured.

And wondering how on earth he could trust himself with her, with her heart, after that. Because he knew now he felt more for Olivia than he'd ever intended or wanted to feel. And never mind all the practical pitfalls of a possible relationship between them, such as the fact she was a Harrington and he was a Chatsfield, or that they lived on different continents and were intent on pursuing their separate careers.

He still was afraid to trust himself with her, with the care and well-being of another person.

Because he was still angry. He'd felt peace in her arms, in her healing touch, but he knew the emotions still churned under the surface.

Because you don't want to admit what you're angry about.

Olivia had probed and pressed about the source of his anger, and he still hadn't told her. Hadn't told anyone, because it shamed him. Because it revealed as much of his character as the anger itself.

But he didn't want to think about that now. He wanted to enjoy what he had with Olivia, for however long it lasted. Smiling, he bent his head and brushed a kiss across her collarbone. She stirred, her eyelids fluttering, and Ben moved lower to her breast. She let out a breathy little sigh and rolled over to give him greater access.

'Now this,' she murmured, her eyes still closed as she hooked a leg around his and drew him to her, 'is a fantastic way to wake up.'

A little while later they were showered and dressed, eating croissants and coffee from room service. 'Any plans today?' Ben asked Olivia, and she shook her head.

'No, thankfully, I've got a day off from schmoozing.'

'I thought you liked the schmoozing.'

She shook her head as she broke a croissant in half. 'I never liked it, but I understand it's necessary.' She smiled ruefully. 'And I've always been willing to do just about whatever it takes to succeed in this cut-throat business.' Her gaze met his. 'Even pretend to have a boyfriend.'

'Well, if you don't have any plans today, what about doing a little sightseeing with me? I've been in Berlin for two weeks and I haven't seen much outside of The Chatsfield.'

Ben watched as a smile blossomed across Olivia's face. 'I'd love that,' she said, and he felt the same kind of smile spread across his own face. Such a small and simple thing…and yet he felt so damn happy.

Even though he knew it couldn't last.

An hour later they walked hand in hand along the terrace of Babelsburg Palace, in the quaint town of Potsdam, a little ways outside Berlin. In February the extensive landscaped gardens were stark and bare, but Olivia could still see the beauty of them, along with the Tudor-inspired palace built by Kaiser Wilhelm. The terraces were scattered with interesting mosaics and sculptures, and they passed a pleasant hour wandering around, chatting about what they saw and enjoying the wintry sunshine.

After they'd seen the palace they retired to one of the many cafés lining Tieckstrasse, sipping espresso and enjoying the warmth.

It had been such an easy, happy day, the kind of day Ben hadn't experienced in for ever. Not as a kid, when he'd been trying so hard to make everything better. Not in the fourteen years since he'd left home, when he'd been bottling up all his emotions, refusing to let anything out, even anything good. And feeling it now, with Olivia, made him realise how precious and important it was.

And in light of that, in the reality of her sitting across from him, blowing on her coffee, her hair curling about her face, his anger was no more than a stumbling block he was ready to cross. He would turn it into a stepping stone.

'I've been angry at Spencer,' he said, blurting the words, surprising both of them. 'My big brother.'

Her lovely brown eyes widened and she lowered her coffee cup, gazed at him with so much trust and confidence his chest hurt. 'Tell me,' she said quietly.

'I told you I was the peacemaker growing up,' he began, feeling for the words, because these realisations were about as new to him as they were to her. 'Always trying to make everybody happy. Always trying to smooth over the arguments.'

'But you couldn't,' Olivia guessed, and he nodded.

'Because it was all a lie. My parents didn't get along because they were both having affairs that they covered up. And my father...my father didn't like Spencer because he wasn't his biological son.'

Olivia's mouth dropped open then, and Ben managed a wry, humourless smile. 'I was shocked too, when I found out.' Shocked and heartbroken.

'And that was when you were eighteen, wasn't it?' she said, and he nodded, both stunned and gratified by her perception.

'My father told me when he was in one of his rages. Drunk too, I think. I couldn't believe it. All this time thinking if I just tried a little harder, we could be a happy family. It was never going to happen.'

'And so you left.'

'It was an impulsive, reckless thing to do, but I didn't know how I could stay. I'd never kept anything from Spencer, and I knew this would destroy him. He'd poured everything into trying to please our—well, *my* father. Wanting to work for The Chatsfield.'

'And you left so he wouldn't find out.'

Ben nodded, his throat turning tight. Olivia leaned forward, her expression so full of compassion that Ben's throat went even tighter. 'So why are you angry at Spencer, Ben?'

'Because…because he never came and found me.' God, he sounded so pathetic, like a whingey little boy. 'Because he let me leave, like I didn't matter to him. And maybe I didn't, because when he came and found me a couple of weeks ago, he told me he's known he's illegitimate for five years.' He heard the naked hurt in his voice and closed his eyes briefly. 'But I'm just as angry at myself, for being so stupid. For trying so hard for so long when there was no point. For caring so much I had to do this great, noble act that was just…useless.' He shook his head. 'For sacrificing myself for my family, and they didn't even care. And,' he finished, trying for wryness, 'for being such a prat about it all, whinging about how nobody loves me.' There. He'd said it all. It felt both good and horrible to be so honest. So vulnerable. And he knew he wouldn't take back a single word…but he wished Olivia would say something in return.

* * *

I love you, Olivia almost said, but then didn't. Everything in her ached to tell him the truth, but the thought of him looking shocked and appalled, of rejecting her, kept her silent.

'Maybe you need to talk to Spencer,' she said instead, feeling wretchedly as if she'd just bowed out of a big moment.

Ben nodded slowly. 'Maybe I do.' He shook his head, let out a wry, self-conscious laugh. 'Sorry for burdening you with all my rubbish.'

'I'm glad you did. I want to hear it, Ben. I want to understand and know you better.' Which was not, Olivia knew, the same thing as saying *I love you*.

But those three words she wasn't so good at saying, especially when it mattered. And Ben probably didn't want to hear them anyway. They hadn't discussed what was between them being anything but the fling they'd originally agreed on.

Really, it was better for her to stay silent. And definitely safer.

Olivia kept up a stream of chatter all the way back to Berlin, trying to keep things light after Ben's heavy confessional…and her backing off.

Back at The Chatsfield Ben was besieged by staff, and Olivia hightailed it to the elevator before they could stumble through any awkward goodbyes. She needed to regroup and think about what she *hadn't* said.

Later that evening, after a restless afternoon of wondering if she dared tell Ben how she felt, Olivia headed up to the pool. She cut through the water, her limbs aching with each stroke. She'd thought a swim might clear her head, but she just felt more tangled up inside than ever.

She loved him, but she had no idea if he loved her back. No clue as to whether he wanted more than the fling they'd agreed on…and she was desperately afraid to ask.

They'd known each other for a little longer than a week, she acknowledged as she pulled herself up onto the ledge of the pool. An intense, amazing week, but still. Falling in love with someone after a handful of days was reckless, to say the least.

But what was a girl to do when a man made love to her with both raw passion and tender sweetness, who wiped her tears away and held her while she cried? Who admitted his own weaknesses and failings with so much heartbreaking vulnerability in his eyes?

How could she not fall in love with Ben, with his dry humour and passion and surprising sensitivity?

Really, this was all his fault.

'We seem to make a habit of meeting here.'

She whirled around, her heart climbing its way up her throat. 'Hey.' Her voice was a croak.

'Hey, yourself.' Ben strode towards her, looking as breathtaking as he did in a tuxedo wearing a pair of swimming trunks. Perhaps even more breathtaking, for she could see his impressive chest and toned abs, trim hips and muscular legs…all of it an incredible, mouthwatering package.

He sat down on the pool ledge next to her, just as he had before, when the paparazzi had taken those incriminating photos.

She gave him a wry smile even though her heart had started to thud and she was so afraid of what he might say. 'Aren't you worried about some photos?' She gestured towards the huge windows overlooking the city. 'Some photographer might be out there, ready to snap something provocative.'

'I'm not worried,' he said, and then he kissed her.

Olivia's mouth opened under his and she clutched at his bare shoulder as heat and happiness flooded through her. Maybe it was going to be okay after all. Maybe she would tell him how she felt, and it would be easy.

He broke the kiss to gaze down at her. 'I'm sorry I was tied up all afternoon.'

'It's okay.'

'I think I needed the time to think,' Ben continued. 'About us.'

Olivia swallowed hard. His tone…his tone didn't sound so good. 'And?' she managed.

Ben shook his head slowly. 'I…I don't know, Olivia. I don't know what I feel for you. I'm still dealing with everything that's come up from returning to The Chatsfield. From knowing you.'

She let out a shaky laugh. 'Glad to be of service.'

'I'm grateful,' he told her seriously. 'I've needed to deal with all that stuff. I need to accept what happened, what I've done. But I don't want to hurt you.'

And he might, if he decided he didn't love her. So she wasn't going to say those three little words after all. 'You won't hurt me, Ben.' She managed a smile. 'I know what this is.' He frowned and she made herself continue. 'Let's just enjoy what we have while we have it, okay? That's all I want.' All she'd let herself want.

Ben's frown deepened, and he stared at her for a moment as if he were going to say something else. Something she was pretty sure she didn't want to hear. Then his expression cleared and he gave her a wolfish smile and said, 'But if there *is* a photographer out there, I don't want to give him an X-rated shot. Let's go somewhere more private.'

Olivia laughed as Ben pulled her up from the side of the pool and drew her towards the sauna.

'Just what kind of private did you have in mind?'

'Private enough,' Ben answered, and kicked open the door.

'Do you have anything...?' Olivia began, and Ben grinned as he pulled a condom from the pocket of his shorts.

'I'm always prepared for emergencies.'

'And is this an emergency?'

'Definitely,' Ben said, and shut the door with the flat of his hand.

Inside the sauna was dim and steamy, and the heat coiled around Olivia as Ben drew her towards him.

'This is a new experience,' she said, her breath catching in her throat as Ben gave her a look full of deliciously sensual intent. 'What if someone comes in?'

In answer Ben turned the lock with an audible click. Olivia let out a rather breathless laugh, and then Ben was gathering her up in his arms and kissing her senseless, that raw passion he'd always possessed surging cleanly to the fore.

The heat and the steam and the dark all combined to make her feel exquisitely aware of every sensation: the press of Ben's mouth to hers, the slippery slide of their bodies and then the deep joy and pleasure of accepting him into her body before they both spiralled towards a shared climax.

There was no anger here, just excitement. Honesty. Passion.

And love, at least on her side, even if she hadn't admitted to it. But she'd take whatever Ben was offering, Olivia knew, and for now it would have to be enough.

Ben slipped from Olivia's bed just after dawn. He didn't want to leave the comforting warmth of her body curled around his, but he hadn't been able to sleep with so much churning in both his mind and gut. Her words echoing in his heart. *I know what this is.*

Yeah. A fling. Two more days of hot sex. Maybe he'd been a fool to think it could become anything else. Anything more.

In the living area of the suite Ben paced restlessly, his hands laced behind his head, the city glittering far below.

He knew he felt more for Olivia than just wanting a fling, but he doubted now whether she wanted to hear it. And he still doubted himself…doubted his ability to keep her cherished and happy and safe.

Maybe he'd never be ready to take that kind of step with a woman. With anyone. People had disappointed him in the past. Maybe that was his fault for having high expectations, but his parents' deception, his brothers' willingness to keep him out of their lives…it had hurt. He knew he needed to make peace with it, find Spencer and talk to him the way Olivia had suggested.

But what about with her? Was he willing, was he ready, to risk his heart and his happiness with her? To have her turn away from him if she didn't feel the same, or it didn't work out between them?

Letting out a weary sigh, Ben turned back to the bedroom. He'd get dressed, leave a note for Olivia and put in a few hours of work before things got crazy. And as for the next two days with Olivia…he'd enjoy them to the hilt, and maybe he'd work up the courage to tell her the truth of his heart.

Just a few hours later, sitting at his desk with a cup of black coffee by his elbow, Ben clicked on his internet browser on his computer and all his hopes blew to dust as he read the news headline blaring from the celebrity gossip section of his homepage.

Starlet's Pretend Boyfriend: Olivia Harrington Made Up Her Romance with Ben Chatsfield!

CHAPTER THIRTEEN

'I'M SORRY, OLIVIA.'

Olivia stared blankly at her agent as the news she'd just imparted registered. She hadn't got the role. After all the drama of her relationship with Ben Chatsfield had been played through the tabloids and gossip sites, the producers had turned to some other actress to play the role that Olivia had hoped would make her career.

'I don't understand,' she said numbly, and Melissa shrugged apologetically.

'I suppose the pretend relationship with Ben Chatsfield backfired. It was too much in the news, fodder for all the gossip sites.'

Olivia closed her eyes briefly. 'Every actor and actress in Hollywood has their life picked over by those sites. It shouldn't cost you a film role.'

'The producers really see this film as a mission. They're passionate about it, and they don't want someone associated with it who's been dragged through the papers.'

'And what happened that was so objectionable?' Olivia demanded. Melissa sighed again.

'Do you really want me to give you a list?'

'We had a photo taken of us in a pool, big deal.'

'Ben shoved you away when you kissed him. It looked…weird. And then the next night you were all over each other, and it was almost too much. And the *next* night Ben nearly punched a photographer—really, Olivia, you have him to blame. The man's a loose cannon.'

'No, he's not,' Olivia snapped. She turned away abruptly, tried to sort through the feelings churning inside her.

She was angry, definitely, but not at Ben or herself. She was angry with the producers, who were putting her through these paces and for what? Nothing, apparently, since she hadn't got the role.

She was disappointed too, Olivia acknowledged heavily, because she'd wanted that role so very much. And yet even as she stood there, everything in her taut and tense, she realised she wasn't nearly as disappointed as she would have expected to be. She wasn't *devastated*.

Which was surprising and a little strange, because acting had been so much about proving herself. To her family. To her mother. But Ben had shown her that you really did have to let go of the past. And securing an amazing role wasn't going to bring her mother back, or atone for her own sins.

Sudden tears stung her eyes as she thought of Ben. They'd spent most of the past twenty-four hours together but they still hadn't talked about the future in any way. She hadn't admitted that she loved him, hadn't had the courage.

She took a deep breath and turned around to face her agent. 'Well, naturally it's a blow, but…'

'Uh-oh.' Melissa was scrolling through her phone and Olivia frowned.

'What?'

'Someone blabbed about the fake relationship,' Melissa said grimly. 'And that really isn't going to be good for your career.' She looked up at her almost accusingly, and Olivia had to bite her tongue to keep from pointing that the fake relationship had been her agent's idea.

'It's in the news?'

Melissa nodded and handed her the phone. Olivia scrolled quickly through the article, picking up the unsavoury highlights. Someone had overheard Ben talking about 'handling the situation.' An unnamed source said Ben had seemed irritated with Olivia, 'hardly a man in love.' And on and on.

It might have been an unnamed source, but Olivia had a pretty good guess as to who had spilled the beans. Ben's crushing-on-the-boss PA.

She handed the phone back to Melissa with a shrug. 'I suppose it was bound to happen.'

'Bound to happen?' her agent repeated, her voice rising. 'Olivia, do you know how this is going to look?'

Olivia planted her hands on her hips. 'Why don't you tell me, Melissa? Since it was your idea in the first place.'

'Only as damage control.'

Olivia shook her head, too tired to argue about it. 'It doesn't matter. What's done is done. And I can guess what it will make me look like— some crazy bimbo who makes up relationships with celebrity chefs.' Thanks to the 'unnamed source,' the article had been just a teeny bit biased against her.

'You don't want people to see you as a joke,' Melissa warned.

'Of course I don't. But I also don't want to jump through any more damn hoops. I've been proving myself to this industry, to everyone, for years, and I'm done. Either I'm a good actress or I'm not. And if someone wants to cast me in their film, they'll cast me because of my talent, not because of some stupid story in the press.'

'It doesn't always work that way, Olivia.'

'Well, it should.' And without another word, she whirled away from her agent and stalked out of the room.

Her cell phone started ringing as she headed downstairs to the lobby to look for Ben. She glanced at the screen and saw it was Isabelle and offered a silent prayer for strength before answering the call.

'Hey, Isabelle.'

'Have you seen the papers?'

'Some.'

'You don't sound very concerned,' Isabelle bit out.

'I'm still processing it,' Olivia answered. 'I only found out five minutes ago.'

'And do you realise,' Isabelle asked frostily, 'how weak and foolish it makes our family look, to have you chasing after a Chatsfield?'

Olivia closed her eyes and took a deep, even breath. 'I wasn't chasing him.'

'That's not what the papers are saying.'

'And since when have you cared what the papers say?' Olivia demanded. 'Or is it only because it's me, the screw-up?'

Isabelle was silent for a beat. 'You're not a screw-up, Olivia,' she said quietly.

'No?' Olivia drew a clogged breath, hating that she was sounding so emotional. 'It's felt that way to me.'

'Why?'

Such a simple question, and yet how could she

answer? 'No one has ever taken my acting seriously. No one except Mom.'

Isabelle was silent for a moment. 'I'm sorry,' she finally said. 'I suppose it always seemed like something you and Mom had together.'

'I miss her,' Olivia whispered, blinking back tears. 'Even now.'

'Oh, Livvy, so do I.'

'I let her down so badly,' Olivia said, her voice squeezed through her throat. 'At the end. You saw how I avoided her…'

'She understood, Olivia,' Isabelle cut across her swiftly. 'She told me once how her being sick was hardest on you, and how sad it made her, knowing she was hurting you.'

'*She* was hurting *me*?'

'She understood,' Isabelle said firmly. 'Trust me. Mom always knew how you felt.'

A tear slipped down Olivia's cheek. She heard the truth in Isabelle's voice, and it finally set her free. She could forgive herself. Her mom had known.

But could Ben forgive himself, truly? He was struggling with the same kind of guilt she was… and he'd told her he was afraid of hurting her. He still didn't trust himself. Still wasn't free.

'I'm sorry if I've been insensitive,' Isabelle said, bringing Olivia back to the conversation. 'I suppose the hotel has consumed me for a long time.' She let out a sad little sigh. 'Maybe too long.'

'How are the negotiations going?'

'Don't ask.'

'I'm sorry if this thing with Ben messes them up,' Olivia said. 'It all kind of spiralled out of control.' In so many ways.

Isabelle sighed again, but this time she sounded both regretful and kind. 'Never mind, Livvy. I'm sorry I've been on your case about it. I'm just really stressed right now.'

Olivia took a deep breath. 'Isabelle, I'll sell my shares to you. I'm sorry I've held on to them for so long.'

'It was a lot to ask…'

'I'm happy to do it.'

'Thank you,' Isabelle said, her voice heartfelt. 'Thank you, Olivia.'

They talked for a little longer, and when Olivia hung up she realised that it had been by far the most honest and important conversation she'd had with a family member in over a decade.

And now she needed to find Ben. She needed to tell him the truth of how she felt—and she wanted to help him find the same freedom she had. That he'd helped her to find.

She headed for his office, and groaned inwardly when she saw his PA give her a triumphant glare. Olivia decided to cut to the chase.

'So how much did the papers pay you to give a tell-all about Ben and me? Not,' she couldn't resist adding, 'that that would have amounted to very much.'

The other woman bristled, but made no pretence as to not knowing what Olivia was talking about. 'Nobody paid me.'

'So why did you do it?'

'Because Ben Chatsfield deserves someone better than you.'

Olivia blinked at the savagery in the woman's tone, but then, to her own surprise, she felt herself soften in sympathy. 'You know,' she told the woman quietly, 'I would have believed that once. I *did* believe that once. But now I know differently. I know I bring out the best in him and he brings out the best in me.' And she wanted to tell him that—and more. She wanted, *needed*, to tell him she loved him.

She'd balked at telling someone she loved her once before. She'd failed her mother because she hadn't been able to handle it, but she wouldn't fail Ben or herself. She'd say the words, even if Ben told her she was on the wrong page or even in the wrong book. She needed to say those words to him for her sake as much as his own, no matter what the outcome.

'Do you know where Ben is?' she asked the

woman, although she didn't hold out much for Petty PA telling her.

In this, however, she was wrong. The PA gave her a smug smile and said, clearly relishing the opportunity to deliver the news, 'He's gone.'

Ben tortured himself by reading just about every article, every salacious snippet, on his imploded pseudo-relationship with Olivia. And in every single one he was made out to be a dupe, and she a voracious and desperate gold-digger.

The anger he felt towards the papers and the snitch, whoever it was, was nothing compared to what he directed at himself.

This was his fault. He hadn't been able to keep up the pretence. He'd failed in some way every time they'd gone out; he hadn't even been able to convince his own PA. No wonder people had figured out it was a lie. And while he didn't really mind coming clean to the whole world about his real relationship with Olivia, he hated the thought of how she looked to everyone. And he knew this would cost her the role that she'd worked so hard for.

He left the office, left The Chatsfield, needing the space. He needed to clear his head and figure out some way to fix this for Olivia.

He walked in a daze towards the Tiergarten, feeling a jarring familiarity in the way things had happened. When his father had told him about Spencer not being his child, their whole family being fake, Ben's first instinct had been to want to fix it. He'd tried to think of a practical solution, and then realised there weren't any.

And now it was happening again. He couldn't fix this. And this time it was all his fault.

He took a long, steadying breath, his mind racing as he tried to find a solution. He could grant an interview to the papers…he could tell them it had all been his fault…he could declare his love for Olivia the way James had with Princess Leila, using a billboard…

None of it, he knew, would get Olivia back her role in this upcoming film. It might even make things worse, and make their not-and-then-real relationship more of a spectacle, or even a joke.

Ben sank onto a bench in the Tiergarten, raking one hand through his hair. He was still playing the peacemaker, he realised, and maybe he needed to stop.

The last time he'd realised he couldn't fix a problem, he'd run away. He'd been afraid and angry and hurt, and that, at eighteen years old, had been his way of dealing with the situation.

But he was thirty-two years old now, and thanks to Olivia, he knew he didn't need to fall back on old patterns of behaviour. He could move on, just as he'd told her he wanted to.

This time, instead of running away from someone else's pain, he was going to run *to*.

His phone rang, and Ben slid it out of his pocket, grimacing slightly as he saw who it was. No big surprise there, really: Spencer was calling, no doubt to give him a piece of his mind about the breaking story.

'Hey, Spencer.'

'Ben.' Spencer's tone was even, but Ben could hear the frustration and anger underneath. Felt the blame.

'I suppose you've seen the papers,' he said.

'Yes.' Ben didn't answer and Spencer continued, 'You've made the Harrington woman look like a delusional idiot.'

Anger sliced through Ben, but he knew that emotion was hiding another. Hurt. 'Do you think that was my intention?' he asked quietly.

'I don't know what your intention was,' Spencer answered, 'but it's not looking good, Ben. We can't offend the Harringtons right now. I told you that…'

'Do you think,' Ben cut his brother off, 'you could back me up just once instead of blaming me?'

Spencer was silent, and Ben could feel his brother's shock even through the phone. Felt his own, because he'd had no idea he'd been going to say that until the words had come out. But once they had he was glad.

'When,' Spencer asked after a long pause, 'have I not backed you up?'

'Why didn't you come find me five years ago, when you'd learned you weren't Michael's son?'

'I…' Spencer was silent for a long moment. 'I suppose I thought you didn't want to be found.'

Ben's throat ached with emotion and he closed his eyes. 'I left when I was eighteen to protect you, Spencer. I knew I couldn't keep the secret from you, and I didn't want you to learn it. Maybe it was the wrong thing to do, a stupid thing to do, but I did it because—because I loved you.'

'Past tense,' Spencer observed with an odd little laugh.

'No,' Ben answered. 'Not past tense. But I've been angry with you. And angry at myself, for being angry at you, because I loved you so damn much.' He'd never imagined he'd be saying this kind of stuff to his brother, and yet he knew he needed to. He *wanted* to. Still, it was hard being this vulnerable, to admit the truth. 'I thought you'd come find me.'

'I thought about it,' Spencer said after a moment. 'A lot. But I didn't know why you'd left, Ben, and I suppose I thought you'd come back.'

They were both silent, absorbing these revelations.

'I'm sorry,' Ben said, 'for leaving.'

'And I'm sorry for being the reason you left,' Spencer answered quietly. 'And for not handling our reunion better. I suppose I wanted to act like we could pick up where we'd left off, but I know we can't. We're two different people now, Ben. And we may be brothers—half-brothers—but we don't know each other any more.' Spencer paused before adding, 'Maybe I shouldn't have asked you to help me out with The Chatsfield. I can see how it would bring a lot of memories back.'

'It did. But that was actually a good thing.' And coming to The Chatsfield had brought him to Olivia, which he never would regret.

And now, he thought as he finished the call and slid the phone into his pocket, he needed to find Olivia.

Ben was gone. Olivia walked out of his office, her mind numb with shock. He'd left without telling her? Was it because of the story breaking? Had everything that had felt so real and honest been nothing more than the charade they'd agreed on?

Maybe she really was as delusional as the papers were making her out to be. She'd come here to tell him she loved him, and he was already gone.

She slowed to a stop in the middle of the lobby, people moving all around her. A lot of people were leaving now that the festival was almost over, and numbly Olivia watched as bellhops sprang to attention and movie stars exchanged effusive goodbyes. She felt separate from it all, isolated from the world she'd tried so hard to belong to.

Totally alone.

'Olivia.'

She stilled, then looked up slowly to see Ben standing by The Chatsfield's front doors. He looked rumpled and sexy and she was so glad to see him that tears started in her eyes.

'Ben…I thought you'd gone. Your PA told me you'd left Berlin.'

'Berlin?' He shook his head. 'No, I just went for a walk.'

Olivia supposed she should have known better than to believe anything his PA had told her. 'I've been looking for you,' she said. 'I want to tell you…'

'I've been looking for you too.' Ben walked towards her, taking long purposeful strides until he stopped in front of her. 'I'm sorry,' he said, and she could see the regret etched in every line of his face. 'I'm so, so sorry.'

Olivia felt as if her heart, along with her hopes, was free-falling towards her toes. She shook her head slowly, wanting to deny his apology. She'd just been about to tell him she loved him, right here in the lobby of The Chatsfield. 'What,' she asked in a scratchy whisper, 'are you sorry for?'

For leaving her? For ending their fling? *For breaking her heart?*

'For causing you to lose your film role.'

She blinked, taking that in, and then she shook her head as relief poured through her. 'Oh, Ben. I don't care about that.'

'You don't care?'

'I lost the film role before the story broke anyway. And I admit I was angry about it for a few minutes, but then I realised I wasn't as disappointed as I expected to be. I was already tired of playing the game, jumping through every hoop to secure a role.' She took a deep breath, wanting to share all she'd learned about herself to him, thanks to him. 'I realised that no film role will atone for the past. I don't want to be someone else just because I'm afraid to be myself.'

'But you're an amazing actress, Olivia.'

'Then producers had better sit up and take notice,' she answered with a smile. 'I want producers and directors to choose me because I'm amazing. Not because I squeezed myself into their mould or played their silly games.' She took another deep breath. 'I'm tired of proving myself. That's something else you helped me to realise. Ever since I let my mother down, I've been trying to prove myself to everyone. My family. Hollywood. I wanted to succeed at acting because I felt as if it would honour her memory and justify my choice to pour myself into it after my mother died. But I'm done with all that.' She met his gaze directly, smiling ruefully. 'And if it means I never act again, so be it.'

'You will act again, Olivia. This will blow over.' He grimaced slightly. 'And I know it's my fault that the whole thing blew up.'

'It was my fault for giving the press the story in the first place.'

'So now we're both to blame.' He reached for her hands, and a thrill ran through Olivia, right down to her toes. 'Olivia…'

'Hold on,' she said, and held up a hand. 'I need to say something first.'

Ben frowned, his hands tensing on hers. 'What do you need to say?'

Olivia took a deep breath. 'That I love you. I don't know how you feel about me, but I know I need to tell you the truth. I kept myself from telling my mother I loved her when she needed to hear it most, and I'm not going to let anyone down like that ever again.' It was impossible to read the expression on Ben's face, so Olivia just ploughed on. 'I love you, Ben. I've been falling in love with you since I first met you. And I know it's only been a handful of days and this whole thing is kind of crazy and I still have no clue if you feel even a tenth of what I do…'

'I do,' Ben interjected, and a smile broke over his face like sunlight. 'I love you, and I was coming to find you and tell you. I spoke to Spencer this morning. I'm…I'm trying to move past everything that happened. Everything I did. I want to move on…with you.'

'Oh, Ben.' Olivia blinked back tears. 'That's the best thing I've ever heard.'

'I know it might be complicated,' Ben told her. 'We have to figure out our families, and the long-distance thing, and it's all happened so fast.'

'Well, as you know,' Olivia teased, 'I'm a leap-before-you-look kind of girl.'

'Then let's leap,' Ben said, and kissed her as everyone around them began to cheer.

* * * * *

*If you enjoyed this book,
look out for the next instalment of*
THE CHATSFIELD:
GREEK'S LAST REDEMPTION
by Caitlin Crews
coming next month.

LARGER-PRINT BOOKS!
GET 2 FREE LARGER-PRINT NOVELS PLUS
2 FREE GIFTS!

H HARLEQUIN®

super romance®

More Story...More Romance

LARGER-PRINT BOOKS!
GET 2 FREE LARGER-PRINT NOVELS PLUS
2 FREE GIFTS!

HARLEQUIN®

Romance

From the Heart, For the Heart

YES! Please send me 2 FREE LARGER-PRINT Harlequin® Romance novels and my 2 FREE gifts (gifts are worth about $10). After receiving them, if I don't wish to receive any more books, I can return the shipping statement marked "cancel." If I don't cancel, I will receive 4 brand-new novels every month and be billed just $4.84 per book in the U.S. or $5.24 per book in Canada. That's a savings of at least 19% off the cover price! It's quite a bargain! Shipping and handling is just 50¢ per book in the U.S. and 75¢ per book in Canada.* I understand that accepting the 2 free books and gifts places me under no obligation to buy anything. I can always return a shipment and cancel at any time. Even if I never buy another book, the two free books and gifts are mine to keep forever.

119/319 HDN F43Y

Name _____ (PLEASE PRINT)

Address _____ Apt. #

City _____ State/Prov. _____ Zip/Postal Code

Signature (if under 18, a parent or guardian must sign)

Mail to the **Harlequin® Reader Service:**
IN U.S.A.: P.O. Box 1867, Buffalo, NY 14240-1867
IN CANADA: P.O. Box 609, Fort Erie, Ontario L2A 5X3

Want to try two free books from another line?
Call 1-800-873-8635 or visit www.ReaderService.com.

* Terms and prices subject to change without notice. Prices do not include applicable taxes. Sales tax applicable in N.Y. Canadian residents will be charged applicable taxes. Offer not valid in Quebec. This offer is limited to one order per household. Not valid for current subscribers to Harlequin Romance Larger-Print books. All orders subject to credit approval. Credit or debit balances in a customer's account(s) may be offset by any other outstanding balance owed by or to the customer. Please allow 4 to 6 weeks for delivery. Offer available while quantities last.

Your Privacy—The Harlequin® Reader Service is committed to protecting your privacy. Our Privacy Policy is available online at www.ReaderService.com or upon request from the Harlequin Reader Service.

We make a portion of our mailing list available to reputable third parties that offer products we believe may interest you. If you prefer that we not exchange your name with third parties, or if you wish to clarify or modify your communication preferences, please visit us at www.ReaderService.com/consumerchoice or write to us at Harlequin Reader Service Preference Service, P.O. Box 9062, Buffalo, NY 14269. Include your complete name and address.

HRLP13R